four rooms

new york

allison
anders

alexandre
rockwell

four
rooms

■

four friends
telling four stories
making one film

robert
rodriguez

quentin
tarantino

Library of Congress Cataloging-in-Publication
Data

Four rooms : four friends telling four stories making one film /
by Allison Anders . . . [et al.]. — 1st ed.
   p. cm.
  ISBN 0-7868-8141-0
  1. Four rooms (Motion picture)   I. Anders, Allison.
PN1997.F5973F68   1995
791.43′72—dc20   95-23300
                                      CIP

Designed by Kathy Kikkert

FIRST EDITION

10 9 8 7 6 5 4 3 2 1

contents

opening

■

MAIN TITLES

As presentation credits begin, we hear Johnny Cash's "Home of the Blues." Then we see Allison's name, under it Alex's, under that Robert's, under that Quentin's, then under that the title logo for Four Rooms, *followed by "Starring Tim Roth as the Bellboy." Then "The Guests" listed in alphabetical order of all the actors playing guests. After the actors' names, we . . .*

FADE UP ON A WALL

The camera pans down a weathered wall covered with postcards from Miami Beach, Florida, the Copacabana, N.Y.C., "Wish You Were Here" from Niagara Falls, rickshaws and babes on beaches, etc. . . .

The camera comes to rest on an old photograph of a 1930s hotel, the "Mon Signor," in its heyday, with a full staff of 30 people posed on the lawn in front.

An Old Guy with a staccato voice delivers a monologue:

> VOICE-OVER
> There used to be a staff of fifty in this place. I'm the only one left from those days. It all comes down to one sap: the night-shift bellhop, that's me. What the hell is a bellhop? You know where the name comes from?
> *(silence)*
> Of course not. . . . It's so simple it's stupid. They ring a bell and you hop. You hop to front and center. No heroes in this line, kid. Just men doing a job. No questions asked, none answered. I try to keep it simple, kid, not too personal. . . .

Another voice of a young man interrupts.

> ### TED
> You met any of those old stars?

> ### THE OLD GUY
> Stars! Are you kidding me? I took Rin Tin Tin out for a shit, for Christ's sakes. I taught Shirley Temple how to roller-skate. I saw Fatty Arbuckle regurgitate three cheese sandwiches right on the spot you're sitting, kid. What did you say your name was?

> ### TED
> Ted.

> ### THE OLD GUY
> Ted, right. I remember Marilyn used to come down at night and doze off in the kitchen. She liked the sound of the fans out back spinning around. Sure, these were stars, kid. Errol Flynn used to call me "Alibi." You'll pick up a few stories yourself, kid.

> ### TED
> I don't think so, not like yours.

> ### THE OLD GUY
> What do you think a star does when he goes to the bathroom, kid?

> ### TED
> Beats me.

> ### THE OLD GUY
> He pulls his pants down and takes a crap just like you and me. Take my word for it.

A wisp of smoke passes over a napkin pinned to the wall with a lip print on it signed "Marilyn." The camera pulls out to reveal Ted and the Old Guy sitting on a foldout cot in a small back room of the Hotel Mon Signor. The old man is dressed in a striped T-shirt with a bellhop's cap on. He looks like an old pirate. Next to him on the bed sits Ted, a young guy with a bellhop jacket draped over his knees. The old bellhop takes a long drag off a big cigar.

THE OLD GUY

Camacho!

TED

Who?

THE OLD GUY

The cigar. Cuban. A good cigar, wrapped in Miami. I got a box of them every Christmas from the chairman of the board. I think he sends them to me to keep my mouth shut. It's tough not to get a little personal in this business.

The old bellhop takes a hit off his cigar and stares down at his cap, lost in thought.

TED

What do you mean?

The Old Guy passes the cap over to Ted.

THE OLD GUY

Put it on.

Ted puts the cap on.

THE OLD GUY

Frankly, you look stupid . . . like the Philip Morris guy. I can't believe I wore that thing for fifty years. You keep it.

The Old Guy gets up from the bed and throws a jacket on. Pulls a few postcards off the wall, throws them in an old straw suitcase, and slams the lid down. He heads for the door. Ted follows.

THE OLD GUY

Stay away from night clerks, kids, hookers, and marital disputes.

The Old Guy pauses for a second and looks Ted dead in the eye.

THE OLD GUY

Never have sex with the clientele.

TED

No way, not me. You got any other advice?

THE OLD GUY

Always get a tip.

The door slams shut on the back room.

INT. HOTEL LOBBY–TWILIGHT

The big empty lobby of the Mon Signor. You can tell that at one time this used to be a swank place. It still is, kinda. It's also kinda decrepit. The concierge—a snappy, fast-talking, red-haired young woman in a blue blazer named Betty—stands behind the reception desk. The old man, suitcase in hand, makes a beeline through the lobby, heading toward the front door. Betty sees him.

BETTY

Sam! Hey, Sam, wait a minute!

The Old Guy stops in his tracks and turns around.

                    THE OLD GUY
What?

Betty comes from behind the desk.

                        BETTY
I just want to say good-bye.

                    THE OLD GUY
Who are you?

                        BETTY
Uhhh, Betty. The concierge. Your boss.

The Old Guy squints his eyes at the young gal.

                    THE OLD GUY
Oh yeah. Gotta light, sister? Goddam cigar went out.

                        BETTY
Yeah, sure.

*She speaks to the Old Guy as she lights his cigar and he puffs
away.*

                        BETTY
I just want you to know, from the owner and all the staff,
your fifty years of service have been an inspiration to us all.
You're a legend in your own time, and the Mon Signor will
never be the—

                    THE OLD GUY
Just forward my cigars, Red.
    (He turns around and walks out, saying over his shoulder)
Aufwiedersehen!

Betty is left standing in the lobby. Ted appears behind her in his bellbody uniform, sans cap.

TED

Sam the bellboy. Now there was a man.

BETTY

Yeah. Oh, hi, Teddy. Ready to start the night shift?

TED

Yeah.

BETTY

Well, let me buy you a drink.

TED

You wanna buy me a drink? I'm starting my shift.

BETTY

You're not an alcoholic, are you; one drink won't kill you.

TED

Yeah, sure.

They walk out of frame. In the empty frame we
SUPER: NEW YEAR'S EVE 7:00 P.M.

INT. BACK ROOM—NIGHT

Betty and Ted sit in the back room, both with drinks in their hand. This dialogue is to be delivered rapid fire, Howard Hawks style.

BETTY

After fifty years, Sam retires, and you're taking over the
night shift.

TED

Correct.

BETTY

You're filling some mighty big shoes.

TED

Oh, I know.

BETTY

Sam was a legend in the hotel business.

TED

Oh, I know . . .

BETTY

A bellhop's bellhop.

TED

An inspiration to us all.

BETTY

He ran the night desk for fifty years, *all by himself*.

TED

An amazing man.

BETTY

No desk clerk. No night man. No help. Just fuckin' Sam,
and his wits.

TED

A man alone.

BETTY

And you're gonna do the same.

TED

I know.

BETTY

Tonight.

Ted spews his drink.

TED

Tonight!

BETTY

Yes, tonight.

TED

I can't.

BETTY

Yes, you can.

TED

No, I can't. I never worked the night shift before.

BETTY

Oh night shift—smight shift.

TED

We were supposed to work it together.

BETTY

I know, but I can't.

TED

Why not?

BETTY

I'm having a New Year's Eve party.

TED

Since when?

BETTY

Actually, I'm not having it. My roommate is. And there's
this guy. German guy, He's gonna be there. And so am I.

TED

I can't run this place by myself.

BETTY

Oh, sure ya can.

TED

No, I can't.

BETTY

Sam ran this place by himself for fifty years.

TED

Yeah, and he had fifty years of fuckin' practice, too. I
haven't had a day.

BETTY

Look, Teddy, calm down—

TED

—Don't call me Teddy.

BETTY

Ted, the night's cake. It's easy. The day's when it's busy.
During the night there's nothing to do.

TED

It's New Year's Eve.

BETTY

Which'll make it less busy than normal. Ever worked on
Christmas? Unless you sell turkeys, business is dead. You
just got butterflies, that's all.

TED

What I have ain't butterflies. I can't handle this hotel all by
myself.

Betty slows the scene down.

BETTY

Okay, let's calm down a minute. Slow it down, cool it off.
Let's just talk.

TED

You can say any goddamn thing you want—

BETTY

—Ted? I thought we were calming down? I thought we were
cooling off? No hostility. Say good-bye to hostility. We're
just talking.

TED

Okay . . . okay . . . okay . . . I'm calm, I'm cool, let's talk.

BETTY

Ted, in a nutshell, all you have to do is hold the fort. It's New Year's Eve. Most of the guests are going out. You'll just be giving them a little nod as they come staggering in at three . . . four . . . five . . . in the morning. Nobody's having any parties, a few get-togethers, but no parties. You got about three people checking in tonight, that's it. The only variable is Chester Rush in the penthouse.

TED

Chester Rush? The guy from *The Wacky Detective*?

BETTY

Yeah, him and his entourage checked in last night. They're in the penthouse. The only reason I refer to it as a variable is that he's a movie star. Ya never know about movie stars. I'm tellin' ya, Ted, it's cake.

Betty takes a piece of paper and writes her number down.

BETTY
(continuing)
And look, if you have any problems, call me at the party.

Ted thinks about it for a moment.

TED

Okay.

BETTY

Great—

TED

—For fifty bucks.

BETTY

Fifty bucks!

TED

You're shirking your duties for this Nazi. For that you pay
a price, and the price is fifty bucks.

BETTY

One, Horst is not a Nazi. Two, that's not a fair price. You're
taking advantage of the situation. Twenty bucks. Now,
twenty bucks is a fair price.

TED

Yeah, but what you're doin' to me ain't fair. And, you are
completely and totally taking advantage of me and your
position. So fifty bucks is the perfect price.

Betty begrudgingly digs in her purse.

BETTY

Okay, but don't be a pussy. You don't bother me unless it's
an emergency. In fact, for fifty bucks, you better not call
unless the fuckin' building's burning down.

She gives him the money.

BETTY

Get ready to take the desk.

Betty leaves.

Ted sits in the chair, takes another drink, and prepares himself for the night.

FADE TO BLACK

STORY TITLE CARD:

allison
anders

room 321

strange
brew

■

FADE IN:

EXT. THE MON SIGNOR HOTEL—DUSK

Ted, the bellboy, meets his first guest of the evening, as a taxi unloads her luggage. To his warm surprise, the guest is a Beautiful Mediterranean Goddess (actually, we will come to see she is not technically a goddess, but a High Priestess). She is about 25 years old, speaks with an Italian accent and is dressed in Gypsy garb. She is Athena.

Ted takes Athena's luggage onto his cart. But one item in a woven Moroccan bag proves to be unbearably heavy. Athena is concerned as he attempts to lift it.

                    ATHENA
          Pleeze be careful—my God. You have no idea . . .

Ted strains as he uses all his cojones to lift the insanely heavy bag onto the cart. Athena tips the cab driver, stingily. The driver winces and gets in the cab. Ted has now managed with grunts and groans and strained blood vessels to put this thing on the cart. The cab skids away. Athena looks at Ted, who is out of breath.

                    ATHENA
          I'm usually a good tipper, but this one—this cab
          driver—he had green all around him. I don't like that in a
          man.

Ted wheezes and pounds on his chest.

                    TED
          Green? Is that bad? Like you read auras or something like
          that?

ATHENA

Something like that.

TED

Yeah, well what color are you seein' around me . . . how's
the tip lookin?

ATHENA

I see purple . . . in your face, and . . .

*As if she can't help herself, Athena's eyes are strangely drawn to
his crotch. She frowns, confused by this impulse. Ted appears to be
charmingly oblivious.*

Athena looks back into his face.

ATHENA

. . . you're okay.

*Ted touches his face—as if searching for the "purple" in it—and
moves the cart inside, discreetly checking out his crotch and giving
her a confused side glance.*

INT. FRONT DESK—DUSK

Ted shifts hats to check the girl in. He checks her reservation.

ATHENA

Athena Z.

TED
(scratching his head—weird name, okay)
You're booked in the Honeymoon Suite—just *one night*?
With all this luggage?

ATHENA

I will only need to stay till sunrise.

TED

Okay . . . and how will you be paying?

ATHENA

With gold.

He looks at this wacky Gypsy chick numbly—she pulls out her Gold Card and smiles.

EXT. ELEVATOR—DUSK

The doors open and Ted and Athena emerge upon the third floor. Ted follows Athena with the cart down the hallway to her room.

AT THE HONEYMOON SUITE DOOR

Ted opens the door, then lifts the easiest bags first. In the center of the room is a Jacuzzi with hokey plastic cupids poised with urns on each side. A dormant fireplace looms beyond the still hot tub.

Ted stares at the heavy bag with anxiety—then looks in front of him to Athena as she rubs the round plastic head of a little Cupid and mumbles, "Perfect." Then, arms open wide, chin lifted to heaven, eyes closed, she mumbles a faint incantation. Then she does a belly-dance wiggle and turns to Ted, who is truly perplexed.

ATHENA

Well—the other bag—I need it.

> ### TED
> Right.

He starts to lift it, again straining and turning purple. He laughs sickly.

> ### TED
> What the hell you got in here, lady? Nuclear weapons?

She relieves him of the task and effortlessly picks up the bag.

> ### ATHENA
> *(dryly)*
> The White Cliffs of Dover.

Ted is stunned as she slings the bag over her shoulder and pauses to pull a 10 spot out of her cleavage. She hands it to him. Ted is grateful and disoriented.

> ### ATHENA
> The others will be coming soon. Send them, pleeze.

Ted nods, confused by "the others," and walks off with the cart. Then he turns from outside the doorway.

> ### TED
> Oh—I forgot to show you how to turn on the Jacuzzi.

But Athena is ahead of him—she flips a switch and water begins to pour from the baby cupids' urns into the hot tub.

> ### ATHENA
> I been in dis' place many New Year's. So . . . you send the others to me, huh. Go now.

As she says this, the door closes with a strange force, shutting Ted
out. Athena takes the bag to the bedroom of the suite.

IN THE SUITE BEDROOM

*A round bed with pink tuck 'n' roll headboard. It's impossible to
imagine having an orgasm in this room—unless it were achieved
by laughing.*

*Athena carefully removes a large, beautiful white slab of stone
from her tapestry bag. She caresses it and carries it like a baby to
the bed and places it in the very center, the head of the rock resting
on dusty heart-shaped pillows.*

*Then she removes from her bag a pink negligée and matching
high-heeled slippers. And these she places with reverence on the
bed.*

> ATHENA
> On this night, oh great goddess Diana, we restore your vir-
> gin flesh and bring you back to real life.

CLOSE ON *the rock slab. We hold on the artifact.*

> ATHENA
> Soon—I take you to the pond for a cleansing. Well, it's a
> swimming pool, but it will be under the setting sun, okay?

INT. FRONT DESK—DUSK FALLS

*Just as Ted is recovering from the mystery of this first guest, El-
speth arrives. She has skin like marble, the body of Venus, piercing*

blue eyes, blond hair, and is dressed all in black clothing, like Honey West in a rubber dress. She carries several bags, and a silver sword on her shoulder.

                         TED
    May I help you?

                        ELSPETH
    I . . . we . . . have a reservation—

Then she snaps, irritated, behind her.

                        ELSPETH
    Kiva!

ANGLE ON *a young punk rocker chick with long orange hair, a long leather coat, wearing a tight T-shirt with studs spelling "PUSSY" across her breasts. This is Kiva.*

Kiva is kicking the tar and nicotine outta the cigarette machine. Just as Ted's eyes grow wide with anxiety, several packs of smokes drop into the juvenile delinquent's hands.

                         KIVA
    Wait up, gawd! I had to get supplies for this boring ass
    night.

                        ELSPETH
                       (to Ted)
    We have a reservation in the Honeymoon Suite.

                         TED
    Oh, yeah . . . you must be one of "the others." And what're
    you carrying—the Rock of Gibraltar?

She stares at him without humor. He fumbles for the key. He walks around the desk to help her with her black crocodile luggage. Jars clang inside. He is ready to go, but Elspeth turns to lecture Kiva on the hazards of smoking, as Kiva lights up.

ELSPETH

What'd I tell you about smoking?

KIVA

You smoke.

ELSPETH

That's right—I smoke, and I'm addicted to it, and I don't want the same thing to happen to you.

KIVA
(In game-show host voice)
"Hello—welcome to this week's edition of the Hypocrite of the Year Award—"

As Kiva goes off on her impression of a game-show host, Elspeth is growing increasingly rageful, like a mother with an unruly child. Ted waits, luggage in hand.

ELSPETH

Kiva! That's enough—

She cuts Kiva's ramble off. Kiva blows smoke defiantly.

KIVA

You're not my mother!

ELSPETH

Yes I am.

KIVA

Then why're we sleeping together?

Ted looks on uneasily at the relationship that is beginning to un-fold here. Elspeth checks his reaction and becomes self-conscious at his scrutiny.

                    ELSPETH
    Well . . . I didn't mean it . . . literally. I . . . I happen to be
    the only one who . . . cares about you—

But her wild child looks off, bored. Elspeth turns to Ted, flustered.

                    ELSPETH
    Please—take us to our room!

Ted smiles uneasily and reaches to relieve her of her sword, but Elspeth quickly slams her palm on the sword and shoots him a piercing glare. He jumps back with a light nervous laugh. He leads the way to the elevator.

AT THE HONEYMOON SUITE DOOR

The couch has been set out here in the hall, as well as coffee tables, lamps, and the TV. Elspeth and Kiva enter the room. Athena is gone. As Ted stumbles around the furniture in the hall, he peers in the room and sees a transformation. With most of the furniture removed, candles and incense and flowers are beginning to form an altar around the fireplace.

But oddest of all is the pink-tinged water swirling in the Jacuzzi and pouring from the cupid urns. A sprinkle of white powder on the carpet encircles the hot tub. Elspeth hands him a tip as he gawks at the circle.

ELSPETH

Flea powder. One of the others is bringing her cat.

Ted starts away again, perplexed. He turns for one last look to see Elspeth kneeling before Kiva, who sprawls on the floor. He shakes his head and leaves.

ELSPETH

You're gonna have to wait in the other room.

KIVA

Why?

ELSPETH

Because I said so.

KIVA

I'll watch TV.

ELSPETH

You can't watch TV because the noise will interfere with our ritual.

Kiva looks around the room and spies the TV in the hallway. She turns to Elspeth with sarcastic concession.

KIVA

Okay . . . Mommy.

Elspeth bristles as the brat saunters off to the bedroom. Elspeth enters the sacred circle, stands before the altar, whips out her sword, and makes a ceremonial gesture pointing the sword upward, perfectly centered between her breasts.

Kiva, behind Elspeth's back, exits from the bedroom doorway into the hall and comes back in, lugging the TV into the honeymoon bedroom.

Elspeth kneels before the altar. Athena enters the room with the "cleansed" artifact and lays the slab in the center of the altar upon the heart-shaped pillows, as Elspeth lays her sword next to the rock. The women look upon the union with tender affection.

ATHENA
Soon—our goddess will come. I will go get her negligée.

Athena stands up but her reverie is dispelled as she shrieks! Loud TV suddenly blasts from the bedroom and Kiva the brat is trying on the pink negligée over her clothes. Athena takes the negligée off the irrepressible youth.

ATHENA
What are you doing! Have you no respect—who—who is dis girl?

ELSPETH

Kiva. My friend. Kiva, turn off the TV! I can't leave her at home—she's on probation and I gotta keep an eye on her.

ATHENA

Well, Elspeth, your *friend* cannot stay here during the ritual. She may be one of your kind, but she is not one of *us*.

ELSPETH

She stays!! Or I go—along with my offering!

The women have a stare-down. Then Athena calls out—

ATHENA

TURN OFF THE FUCKING TV, MAN!

KIVA

(in a seductive pout)

Make me . . .

Elspeth becomes anxious with jealousy. Athena is exasperated as she firmly demands from Elspeth—

ATHENA

Let's not forget—I am the High Fucking Priestess. Deal with dis girl!

Elspeth defers to Athena with remembered reverence and respect. She bows apologetic and scurries to the bedroom.

ATHENA

(eyes lifted to heaven, wearily)

Tell me—did we have deeze problems in Salem? I don't think so . . .

IN THE BEDROOM

Elspeth swallows her rage and approaches the brat with a soft touch.

ELSPETH

Kiva . . . you know what I love about you?

Kiva smirks . . . yeah, she knows.

ELSPETH

Your sweet side.

KIVA

And what do I get if I'm sweet?

ELSPETH

You get whatever you want. And you know what else I love about you?

KIVA
(seduced now)

What?

ELSPETH

Your nose.

And saying this, she kisses Kiva's nose and leaves the room. Kiva is quieted now. As Elspeth closes the bedroom door, she has the last word.

ELSPETH

And I saw you checking her out.

Kiva slinks back on the bed, put in her place—for now.

IN THE HALLWAY/EXT. ELEVATOR—DUSK

The doors open and Ted pushes a cart of expensive designer luggage—and lots of it—behind yet another Gorgeous Gal. This one is Jezebel, a Southern beauty, fawning over her cat, as she carries nothing else, and proceeds down the hall like a Southern princess.

JEZEBEL
(talking to her cat in baby talk)

Oh you little stinker . . . oh you sweet little muffin. Yes . . . Mama loves the baby.

AT THE DOOR

Jezebel bursts in, chattering.

JEZEBEL

Well, this is just darlin'! Just darlin' Hi-dee, girls . . .

Ted carries all her bags inside awkwardly. Again, the place has become all the more transformed with wild canopies of exotic cloths and fixings. Elspeth and Athena are hard at work on a strange nature sculpture as Jezebel enters. She stands inside the powdered circle and before the hot tub, which now has dark blue water swirling inside. She presents her cat—upward toward heaven—frees the cat, bares her breasts, and sucks in the vibes: "Ahhhh."

Ted settles the bags down, hoping for a peek at her charms, but her back is to him. The kitty rubs on her leg. She picks it up and presses it against her bare breasts, petting it sweetly. She winks and hands him a tip.

> JEZEBEL

Toodle-loo.

And saying this, she shoos him away. Through the glass doors to the bedroom, she sees Kiva sprawled on the bed, writing on herself.

> JEZEBEL

Well—I see Elspeth has herself a new lil' fool—what the hell is she doin' here on our night of annual ritual?

> ATHENA
> *(wearily)*

I have sanctioned her presence, as long as she behaves. Come on—there is more work to be done to welcome our great Diana.

> KIVA

I WANT ROOM SERVICE!!

> ELSPETH

Why do I always attract girls who are looking for a baby-sitter?

JEZEBEL

Well now, honey, maybe Juvenile Hall ain't the best place
to find serious relationship material.

Elspeth seethes at her. Jezebel acts blithely innocent.

IN THE HALLWAY

*Ted is walking from the room with the cart. His face is etched in
a mask of perpetual frown as he looks at the tip in his hand—at
least these lunachicks tip well.*

*Waking him out of his deep mood is Raven. Another female intoxi-
cation, she wears a short skirt, all done up in Native American,
Southwestern themes. No shoes. But she carries a small, old hand-
made broom. She moves down the hall, blissed-out. Ted makes eye
contact, despite himself.*

RAVEN

I'm looking for the room for making love.

TED

You might be referring to the Honeymoon Suite. Straight
thata way . . . you can't miss it—see all that furniture in
the hallway—

RAVEN

Oh I know the way. I just wanted you to know that I knew
where I was going and that you needn't bother yourself with
me. The others are here—great!

TED
(wearily)
Oh yeah—it's so great—it's fantastic.

RAVEN
(in deep empathy)
Ohhh . . . I know it all seems very strange but you're coping
with us much better than the bellboys of past New Year's.

TED
Past New Year's?

RAVEN
Oh yes—we've been coming here every New Year . . . for a
long time. Thanks for your patience.

TED
Oh hey—no problem—wreck the place. Bring in cats. Ruin
the carpet with flea powder, pour paint in the Jacuzzi.
Throw the furniture out the . . . where're your bags?

RAVEN
I travel very light.

*Ted looks down at the broom at her side, her bare feet, her thick
dark hair. It keeps getting weirder. She wanders off.*

INT. FRONT DESK—NIGHT

*The last of the lovely girls arrives. She is different from the others.
She looks like a farm girl, very Earth Mother, with a tablecloth
halter top and skirt, sandals, and a simple scarf over her long
dark curls. She carries two bags by herself and holds a small black
pot under her arm. She is Eva.*

TED
(already weary of these girls)
Yeah, yeah, Honeymoon Suite.

EVA

Oh . . . yes . . . I'm late.

She lowers her eyes, worried.

TED

All right—lemme give ya a hand.

EVA

Oh . . . no, that's all right. I can carry them by myself.

She is so sweet and sincere that he feels like a heel to have been irritated with her. He picks up her bags.

TED

I'm a man doin' a job—no hero.

Eva smiles, beautifully.

EVA

Well gosh—thank you!

IN THE ELEVATOR

Ted holds Eva's hippy sacks as she holds her black pot. There is a shy quiet tension here.

EVA

Tell me, how long have the others been here?

TED

About an hour.

Eva's heart sinks. They arrive at the door. He carries her bags in.

IN THE SUITE

The room is entirely transformed into a beautiful glowing palace with an elaborate altar, both earthly and other-earthly. The other four girls are arranging the altar as Eva enters.

ATHENA
You are very late, Eva.

EVA
I'm sorry, Athena. I was attending a birth and the placenta was late in coming.

Ted is slightly queasy. She hands him a tip and smiles, then takes it back.

EVA
Oh, wait, lemme give you a little more than that . . .

Ted's no fool, he waits while Eva looks through her change purse.

ELSPETH

Which birth is more important to you, that of a mortal or that of a goddess?

EVA

All life is precious . . . but I do apologize for being late, Elspeth.

JEZEBEL

Back home they jist yank on the umbilical cord, do a Karate chop on the mama's belly, and them things come right out.

EVA

They do that here, too, Jezebel, in the hospitals, but it causes hemorrhages. I fed the mother a bowl of comfrey tea and it brought the afterbirth down perfectly. The couple are going to use it for fertilizer to plant a lovely tree for their baby.

KIVA

Oh wow—if they were really back-to-nature they'd eat it, like other mammals do.

CLOSE ON *Ted's face as he gets thoroughly grossed out.*

RAVEN

In some Native American cultures, they dry the umbilical cord, grind it to a fine powder, and put it in a leather pouch that the baby wears to ward off evil. But burying the placenta is also a very sound ecological practice—'cause of the oxygen it carries.

EVA
(cheerfully to the others)
Yes—because you see when the placenta detaches from the uterine wall . . .

TED
(wincing in disgust)
Uh, thank you, ladies—I'll be going now. If you need anything—

Eva places a nice tip in his palm.

ATHENA
Wait. We do need a few things.

*Ted sighs as Eva enters the circle with her black pot. She kneels
softly, holds her hands in piety before the altar, and softly incants
as she offers her pot and places it on the altar. The stone and
sword and flowers now rest here on pillows covered in chiffon
scarves. The negligée hangs from the mantel, the slippers underneath as if expecting someone to materialize into the garments.*

ATHENA
We need fresh rosemary from the kitchen. Mostly what we
need is from the kitchen. Hey, are you listening?

Ted is watching Eva, enchanted.

TED
Yeah, yeah, rosemary.

ATHENA
And a little bit of sea salt or Kosher salt if you don't got no
sea salt. A bottle of spring water—Italian please, not
French shit.

KIVA
And some french fries!

ELSPETH

Kiva, shut up.

ATHENA

(irritated)

And some ginger, two of the eyes of a trout fish, and a piece of raw meat, liver if you have it.

KIVA

(whining)

I want fries—you dumb jerks with your stupid fucking ritual!

ATHENA

Shut up, you little shit.

ELSPETH

Don't talk to her that way!

Ted has scribbled the items down as she speaks. He looks at this list and these girls and shudders as he walks away. He turns, points at Eva.

Ted smiles at this angel of a girl. She smiles back. But, as she looks him in the eyes, he feels a strange buzzing connection happening. He holds his head, almost swooning with dizziness. Athena smirks.

ATHENA

Get to work, man.

Ted comes out of his daze, looks at the list again and huffs off. After he goes, the girls begin to bring forth their most treasured offerings in ornate ancient bottles, vases, or vials.

Jezebel folds her arms and clears her throat in the direction of Kiva, sitting idly on the edge of the blue water Jacuzzi, with her feet dipping irreverently in the water.

ELSPETH

Kiva . . .

KIVA

What?

ELSPETH

You have to go in the next room now.

KIVA

Oh wow, like I'm bummed out that I can't watch.
(*whining at Elspeth*)
I'm bored!

ELSPETH

UP!

She climbs up the stairs, trying to pull the brat to her feet.

KIVA

Don't put me in there by myself. I'll miss you way too much.

ELSPETH

Kiva, don't do this to me.

Kiva sees a bit of weakening here; she takes her feet out of the Jacuzzi. She begins to speak softly.

KIVA

Please . . . if you just lemme . . . I'll play dress-up with you, the way you like it . . . you know what I mean . . . remember . . . ?

Elspeth begins to weaken. But continues to pull the brat up. Kiva pours on softer seduction.

KIVA

We can pretend and I'll do it exactly . . . the way you want it . . . with the egg whites and the kilt.

Elspeth is now fully seduced. Kiva takes Elspeth's hand and presses it lightly on her face.

ELSPETH

You mean . . . like last week?

Kiva nods. Elspeth is enthralled, but from a disgusted "ick" sound from Jezebel, Elspeth realizes she's revealing this side of her life—in front of her coven. She nervously looks around and sees all the coven looking at her: a disgusted Jezebel, an understanding Raven, a preoccupied Eva, and an impatient and stern Athena.

Elspeth comes to her senses, straightens her posture.

ELSPETH

We'll talk about this later, Kiva.

KIVA

(angrily)

No!

She turns on Elspeth and bites her hand. Elspeth pulls her arm away and grabs Kiva by the hair.

JEZEBEL

Aw, really now—child abuse?

ELSPETH

You stay outta this!

ATHENA

I demand this stop now, Elspeth!

Elspeth lets go of Kiva's hair. Kiva jerks away from her.

KIVA

I'm running away from you!

ELSPETH

Fine. Go ahead. And I'll call your parole officer and she'll find you and send you back to Eastlake!

Kiva stomps off into the bedroom.

ATHENA

Now that the fucking melodrama is over, can we start the goddamn ritual—*pleeze?*

Elspeth enters the powered circle. Each girl takes off her shoes. They anoint themselves with oils.

ATHENA

We are communing here on New Year's Eve to bring to life
the great goddess Diana, who was turned to stone in this
very room forty years ago today.

*The girls moan in sleepy, eerie agreement as they begin to sway
within the circle.*

ATHENA

Diana, great beautiful one, we make these offerings to you,
that we may undo the wicked spell which deprived you of
the seed of your lover, your virginal blood, of your very life.
We now form the symbolic rock with our bodies.

*And saying this, the girls all form a "rock" with their bodies
gracefully draped one upon the other. Music begins, and slowly
they start to unfold from the rock. The girls each find their place
in a semicircle around the Jacuzzi. Some bare their breasts, others
strip off a layer of clothes. They anoint their arms with water from
the Jacuzzi.*

*They begin a lovely dance, snaking their way around the semicir-
cle. The first one to go from one end to the other is Athena. She
then proceeds up the stairs and positions herself between the altar
and the Jacuzzi. She steps forth with a bottle to the altar and pours
it into the Jacuzzi.*

ATHENA

On this night, in this hour, we
Call upon the Ancient Power
O Goddess bride, I offer thee
Milk from a mother's sweet titty!

Each of the girls moans eerily. Athena places the bottle on the altar and bows away. She joins the circle as Elspeth now steps forward with her offering in a vial.

ELSPETH

To reverse the evil which has been done
I make this offering to the Divine One
A whore not, an innocent was,
For whom I seized a virgin's blood.

JEZEBEL

Goddess of Light, Goddess of Lust
To undo this awful spell is a real must.
To bring you life and get you high
I offer the sweat of five men's thighs.

The girls moan loudly as they sway. Jezebel places her offering in the hot tub and bows out, returning to the circle. Now Raven comes forth with a small leather canteen. She unscrews the lid as she offers in her opiate stupor.

RAVEN

Diana, oh great one, we live without sun
Until this wicked curse is undone.
In hope that you live, and to us appear,
I have collected a year's worth of tears.

She pours liquid into the mix, as the witches moan. Now it's Eva's turn. Eva continues to sway, not moving forth to the altar. The girls keep their eyes closed as they sway, waiting for Eva's offering. Athena finally gives her a push and she goes.

Eva kneels before the altar. She produces a silver bottle with a chain on its cap and neck. She timidly begins to incant.

EVA

Great Goddess Diana, fail you I will,
I was to bring fresh sperm from my Bill.
I had him erect, and his semen would follow
But alas I was hot, so hot that I swallowed.

The moans turn to wails as the girls GASP and SHRIEK! Athena opens her eyes, wildly.

ATHENA

You stupid little witch! You swallowed the sperm? Aye—yi—yi!

Elspeth opens her eyes and folds her arms, smirking bitterly.

ELSPETH

It just shows what an amazing lack of control you have over yourself, Eva!

JEZEBEL

Honey, why didn't you just use your hands? Didn't your mama teach you not to put them things in your mouth?

RAVEN

I understand though . . .

Eva bursts into tears. Athena is firm.

ATHENA

There is no time to cry over swallowed sperms. You're gonna have to get some, baby. You have one hour to prove what kind of witch you really are.

Just then: a knock at the door.

ATHENA
(calling out)

What do you want!

TED

Ted . . . the bellboy.

Athena smiles and turns to Eva.

ATHENA

Mr. Bellboy, come right in!

Ted opens the door. His eyes bulge out as he looks upon the fleshly
feast. He steps back. They giggle seductively, all except Eva, who
sniffles, red-eyed. Amazingly, Ted's attention is captivated by
Eva's sorrow, not by the naked charms of the other witches. She
shyly covers her breasts. Sensitive to her shame and sorrow, he
looks away and steps from the door to fetch the room-service cart.
Athena directs the others to put on their shirts. Ted wheels in the
cart.

TED

Here's the things you asked for. Oh, and uhh, sorry, but I'm not gonna pick the eyes outta this dead fish.

He points to the trout. Elspeth picks it up, flings the eyes into the Jacuzzi, and tosses the trout out of the window. She smirks at him contemptuously.

ATHENA
(handing Ted 50 bucks)

Okay, mister, here's your fifty-dollar tip, only, you have to do one more thing . . . make our little Eva smile. Can you? We'll leave you alone.
(to Eva, firmly)
And don't use your mouth!

The girls step out. Athena turns to Eva and points to her watch, then holds up one finger. Eva looks up, worried. The door closes on her and Ted. She looks at Ted and sighs. He covers her with a shawl.

IN THE HALLWAY

The other witches listen at the door.

ELSPETH

If she doesn't get his goop in ten minutes, I'm going to take him myself.

JEZEBEL

Ha! That'll be a first fer you.

ELSPETH

Oh shit—Kiva!

She runs back in for her bratty girlfriend, who is already sneaking out the bedroom door.

ELSPETH
And just where do you think you were going?

KIVA
Well, gawd—I need a candy bar or something—you haven't
fed me all day. I'm getting all shaky. My blood sugar's
really low.

JEZEBEL
Elspeth—honestly now—some baby-sitter you're turnin'
out ta be!

ATHENA
Enough, girls. I will collect fresh earth. Jezebel, I want you
to gather damp moss. Raven, you bring me a birch branch.
Elspeth you go feed your terrible girlfriend. We meet back

here in one hour and let's all have faith that Eva can get this guy off.

The witches disperse.

INT. HONEYMOON SUITE—NIGHT

Eva sits among pillows before the altar as Ted stands in front of her. Ted is trying his best to make poor Eva smile. But no matter what his antics, she looks off sadly.

> TED
>
> Help me out, lady, I gotta earn this fifty bucks!

> EVA
>
> Oh look, they don't care if I smile or not! All they want is . . .

Ted waits; she sighs, and rests her chin in her hand.

> EVA
>
> You wouldn't understand, believe me.

She begins to cry tearfully again.

> TED
>
> Try me. I've been around, y'know.

He postures proudly, all puffed out. Eva looks at him helplessly. And he paternally encourages her to explain.

> EVA
>
> Well . . . okay. The five of us—Elspeth, Jezebel, Athena, Raven, and me—are a coven.

TED

Ha, like a coven of witches?

EVA

Yes.

TED

(stunned)

Oh.

He looks around the room: QUICK CUTS of candles, iconography, jars of lurid substances, unknown body parts of animals woven into the nature sculpture . . . and are those tongues in that can? Ted's getting the creeps, but again puffs himself up.

TED

I knew that!

EVA

(getting calmer)

And you see, our coven has spent forty years trying to perfect a ritual to undo a wicked curse put on our goddess Diana.

TED

Gee, you don't look a day over twenty!

EVA

Oh . . . ha ha . . . I mean the witches before us tried and failed. But Athena, our High Priestess, discovered a great potion to reverse the evil spell which turned our beautiful goddess into an old rock.

TED

(looking at the rock)

Yeah? Is . . . is that her?

Eva nods, looking lovingly at the stone.

> EVA

She was a beautiful virgin. An entertainer by trade, but a great sorceress by design. It was here in this very room, on her wedding night, a jealous rival placed the curse on Diana.

> TED

She turned to—that—here?

> EVA

Yes . . . and her young husband turned into a pink fish! They found him swimming in the pool in circles. While our dear goddess: a stone in her honeymoon bed.

Ted frowns as he ponders all this. Eva takes a photo from the altar and hands it to Ted.

> EVA

This was Diana.

CLOSE ON *photo: a Blond Bombshell in full-on Betty Page attire, a bare-titted pinup girl, playfully spanking a girl in bondage with a spiked high heel.*

> TED

This girl here? This is the goddess Diana?

The photograph slowly comes alive. Diana stops spanking the girl and unties her. She pulls the girl (in the black satin mask) up off her lap and makes the girl stand. The women face each other and break into a cheek-to-cheek tango.

CLOSE ON *Ted as he shakes his head. Are his eyes playing tricks on him?*

TED

I hate to tell you this, but I kinda doubt she was a virgin.

EVA

Oh, but she was! She had lovers, but she saved *that* for marriage. Which is the example I've tried to follow: to do everything but *that* till I marry . . .

She begins to sob again. Ted comforts her.

TED

Hey, don't cry . . . a virgin is a rare and beautiful thing. If you say she was a virgin, I'll believe it.

EVA

Well, it doesn't matter now . . . and she won't be resurrected tonight 'cause I failed her. I let my whole coven down!

TED

Wait a sec—that rock was gonna turn back into *this*?

He holds up the photo. Eva nods.

TED

Now, that would be something worth seeing!

EVA

Only, not now—we were each supposed to bring some-thing—a life fluid.

TED
(wincing in disgust)
If this is gonna be like one of those afterbirth conversations, I don't think I wanna hear this.

EVA

Only . . . I swallowed it . . .

TED

You swallowed what?

Eva looks off. Ted searches his brains, thoroughly sickened now.

TED

You mean, you were supposed to bring . . . like . . . like a
guy's . . . and you . . . ?

She nods; he winces, queasy. Eva looks at him, helpless.

EVA

And now, you're my last chance!

TED
(laughing)

Yeah, sure.

TED
(then—panic)

Whoa, what? You want my—for the—witchy poo—ahh
no—no way—nope. Besides, it's against hotel policy. I was
warned: "No sex with the clientele"!

*Eva sobs, pleading. She throws off her shawl, baring her lovely
breasts, and reaches her arms around his neck. He keeps backing
off. Unbeknownst to him, he is already doing a ritualistic shuffle.*

TED

Ha, c'mon now, joke's over.
(Seeing this is no joke)
Hey, we're gonna step in the flea powder.

EVA

That's not flea powder, that's sacred dust ground from the horns of Albino goats.

TED

Right! I knew that!

He is backing away, into the circle, as she comes for him, soft and sweet. Her eyes are again putting the magic hex on him, as he tries to resist her gaze.

TED

What's a nice girl like you doing in a coven, anyway?

EVA

Well, see, what I really want to do is be a midwife. I've attended four births already! I can prevent vaginal tears and everything.

TED
(trying to dodge her hexing eyes)
Well, that's a good thing! A guy doesn't like surprises down there.

All the while she is stepping toward him into the circle.

EVA

I joined the coven to attain greater understanding of my feminine power so I could become a truly great midwife!

TED
(the hex working now)
Oh, well, I see you've been gaining a lot of insight into your . . . girl powers . . .

Eva sweetly takes his hand and places it on her breast.

> EVA
>
> Do you really think so?

> TED
> *(buckling under the temptation)*
> Well, yeah, I'd say that seems to be the case. . . .
> *(She licks his neck; his eyes roll back heavenly)*
> Ohhh, God! Betty's gonna kill me!

> EVA
>
> Who's Betty—your girlfriend?

> TED
>
> No. My boss.

> EVA
>
> Oh good!

> TED
>
> Oh no!

They fall into a kiss, as she begins to remove his cap. She moves him toward the Jacuzzi, closer and closer.

DISSOLVE TO:

INT. HALLWAY—NIGHT

Ted pushes his room-service cart out. He is flushed. Puffed up. Lights a cigarette, takes a great big, satisfied drag. Eva runs to

*the door dreamily, her naked body wrapped in her shawl. She
passes him a card.*

                          EVA
        My phone number in Topanga. Call me?

                          TED
                        (cocky)
        Sure, baby. Yeah, I'll give ya a call.

*She smiles and shuts the door. The other witches are arriving with
supplies from the garden. Kiva, now having raised her blood
sugar, sucks on a lollipop, a sunny girl. She talks to Raven, who
carries a birch limb.*

                          KIVA
        What's that used for?

                         RAVEN
        It's a birch branch, symbolizing eternal life. You can also
        use the bark for a tea which assists in astral travel.

                          KIVA
        Hey—I wanna be a witch!

*The other girls roll their eyes as Elspeth smiles proudly. Ted blows
smoke at them and pushes his cart off down the hall. The witches
run inside the room.*

IN THE SUITE

Eva sits, blissed-out, in the center of the circle, smiles.

                          EVA
        I'm a woman now!

ATHENA

But where is his "stuff"?

EVA
(pointing to the Jacuzzi)
We did it right there, in the big cauldron!

JEZEBEL

Ooohhh honey, you're gonna be sore tomorra! Didn't your
mama teach you that water strips a girl's lubrication?

RAVEN

Sex in water is great in the movies, not in real life . . . but
you will learn. As we all did.

JEZEBEL

Yeah, when she can't walk . . .
(to Elspeth)
I guess you wouldn't have those kinds of problems—
without penetration.

ELSPETH

No. And virtually no cervical cancer, either.

ATHENA

Okay, girls, enough Sex Education 101, let's get going with
our ritual, goddammit.

*Athena regally leads the ritual as they all bare their breasts again.
Kiva throws off her shirt to join in. As she does, we see black
bondage tape on her nipples. Elspeth darts a quick look at the
tape, looks at the other witches—not sure she likes this—but she
goes with it. The witches sway in a circle, eyes closed, as Eva
makes her offering.*

EVA

Goddess Diana, I offer you
The jism of the one I wooed for you
That you may live and know such bliss
Of getting laid by a guy like this.

The witches all incant.

ALL OF THE WITCHES

So must it be.
Three times three times three.

They march half-naked as they moan and revel in eerie cries. The Jacuzzi begins to bubble and boil. Their cries heighten; the potion bubbles over.

DISSOLVE TO:

HOURS LATER

Athena reads from a huge leatherbound book, The Book of Shadows, *full of potions and spells. Four discouraged witches pack their bags. The room has been restored to its worldly under-splendor. Kiva uses the remote on the TV . . . so much for witchcraft. The slab of rock remains a slab.*

ATHENA

I don't understand what went wrong.

ELSPETH

I say Eva pulled one over on us.

EVA

What?

JEZEBEL

Honey—Eva was wearing the face of someone just fucked good . . . and the best actress in this world, or any other, can't fake a thing like that!

ELSPETH

Exactly—if she was fucked so good, how could she save his come?

RAVEN

It could be done . . .

ATHENA

Girls, knock it off.
(She looks up from the book)
Maybe . . . maybe it needed to be the sperm of a virgin male.

EVA
(dreamily)

He was no virgin!

The witches sadly collect their things. Athena, deep in thought, strokes the slab.

ATHENA

Let's leave her here, with the sword, until dawn. I will come back for her before checkout time. I just . . . feel too sad to carry her away before the sun comes up to warm her.

They all agree. They pick up their bags and head out.

JEZEBEL
(cuddling her cat)

I can't believe we have to carry our own bags out! My mama would have a hissy fit!

KIVA
(flirtatiously)
I'll carry your bags.

ELSPETH
(firmly)
You're carrying *my* bags!

They leave the room. Jezebel's cat leaps from her arms as she hoists her luggage. Eva walks out satisfied, though perhaps already a little sore—"ouch," she says, and smiles. Athena takes one last look at their goddess slab.

ATHENA
Next year, we try again—with virgin sperm.

She closes the door on the Honeymoon Suite (till next New Year's Eve!).

FADE TO BLACK.

four rooms

FADE UP ON:

INT. MON SIGNOR LOBBY—NIGHT

Ted behind the desk, on the phone. We only hear his side.

TED
Oh, Jesus, what did I tell you? Do you want milk and cookies, or do you not?

(pause)
I can't turn on an adult station without permission from
your parents.
(pause, he checks his computer)
That's not what the machine tells me.
(pause)
You be good and you'll get milk and cookies, but for now
leave me alone, please. I'll be up later to put you both to
sleep.

He hangs up.

                         TED
                    (to himself)
Goddamn kids.

SUPER: *1:00* A.M.

The phone rings again.

                         TED
Room Service.

INT. ROOM 404—NIGHT

*A small party is going on. A long-haired Yuppie Scum type is on
the line. Music BLARES. People dance in background.*

                    YUPPIE SCUM
What room am I in?

INT. FRONT DESK—NIGHT

BACK AND FORTH

>   TED
> This is the front desk, sir.

The Yuppie turns away from the phone and speaks to Real Theodore.

>   YUPPIE SCUM
> What room are we in?

>   REAL THEODORE
> How should I know? I just got here.

>   YUPPIE SCUM
>   *(into phone)*
> You know, don't you have one of those light things?

>   TED
> If you care to go to the door and look on the other side,
> you'll find the room number.

>   YUPPIE SCUM
>   *(To Real Theodore)*
> Call my assistant and ask her what floor we're on.

>   REAL THEODORE
> Who's your assistant?

>   YUPPIE SCUM
> The girl you party with every night.

                    REAL THEODORE
                      (to himself)
Who?

                         TED
I'm here alone, sir.

                    REAL THEODORE
It's room 404, I think.

                       YUPPIE
I could have sworn we were on the fifth floor.

                    REAL THEODORE
Right. 404.

                     YUPPIE SCUM
                      (into phone)
Right. 404.

                         TED
What do you need, sir?

                     YUPPIE SCUM
                   (to Real Theodore)
What do we need?

                    REAL THEODORE
Ice.

                     YUPPIE SCUM
Ice?

                    REAL THEODORE
Ice.

YUPPIE SCUM
(into phone)

Ice.

TED

Ice.

YUPPIE SCUM

Yeah. Ice.

TED

Right, sir. Ice. 404. I'll be with you momentarily.

CUT TO:

STORY TITLE CARD:

alexandre
rockwell

room 404

the
wrong
man

■

INT. DARK HALLWAY

Ted saunters down a hallway with a butt hanging out the corner of his mouth and a bucket of ice swinging at his side. He pulls up at a door on which the faded numbers read something like "Room 404."

Ted knocks on the door. After a moment, the latch is thrown and the door swings open. Ted cautiously steps into the dark room.

INT. ROOM 404

> TED
>
> Anybody home?

A DEMONIC CACKLE *cuts through the darkness.*

> MAN'S VOICE
>
> No one here but us chickens.

> TED
>
> Say, it's pretty dark in here, sir.

> MAN'S VOICE
>
> What do you expect, Theodore, a fuckin' floor show?

> TED
>
> Do I know you?

> MAN'S VOICE
>
> I don't know. Do you?

In a flash the lights switch on and Ted finds himself staring down the barrel of a pretty intense-looking .357 Magnum, cocked and ready to fire. At the other end of the gun stands a 50-year-old man, Sigfried, who sports a Cheshire Cat smile and a "just try fuckin' with me" look on his face. Sigfried isn't the only person in the room. Directly behind him sits a beautiful young woman, Angela, gagged and bound to a chair. Ted drops the bucket to the floor.

TED

I brought your ice.

SIGFRIED

That's cute. In fact, the whole getup's kind of cute. The monkey suit's a nice touch, honey puss.

TED

This has to be a mistake. Is this room 404?

SIGFRIED

Theodore? What do you take me for, Theodore?

TED

A very upset man?

Sigfried reaches in his pocket and throws a handful of assorted stimulants into his mouth, chewing on them like they were breath mints. Sigfried thrusts his hand forward, gripping Ted by the throat, and leads him to Angela.

SIGFRIED
(to Angela)

I am an upset man, Theodore.

TED

How do you know my name, sir?

SIGFRIED

I'm psychic, Theodore.

TED

Look my name is Ted, actually, and I have no idea what's going on here, but obviously I've come at a bad time.

SIGFRIED

Let's not belabor the fact that you have no sense of timing, Theodore. The fact is you're here.

Sigfried turns to Angela.

SIGFRIED
(continuing)
And I couldn't think of a better time for you to introduce
me to your beau than on New Year's Eve.

TED
Oh fuck, there's a mistake. You're fucking wrong here. My
name is Theodore, yes! My mother named me that and I
hate the name. But I'm a fucking bellhop. People call me
Ted. I work here.

*Suddenly, with great force, Sigfried slams the butt of his pistol
smack into Ted's temple, sending him to the floor. Ted looks up at
Sigfried in shock.*

SIGFRIED
Look, I'd love to sit here all night with you talking about
things like when you broke in your first mitt—
(pause)
That was insensitive of me, wasn't it, T H E O D O R E?
But let's cut to the chase, okay?

TED
Okay.

SIGFRIED
So apologize!

*A tense silence fills the room. All eyes are on Ted, who can't figure
what the fuck this guy wants.*

TED
For what?

Sigfried looks hard with disbelief at Ted, who winces back.

SIGFRIED

You are really beginning to annoy me, Theodore.

Sigfried throws another handful of pills into his mouth.

TED

Look, obviously you two are working something out and if I could help you with your problem I would.

SIGFRIED

What are you saying? Are you saying I got a problem? Are you trying to say I don't give her what she needs? That I'm FUCKING INSENSITIVE!

TED

Look, is this about another man? Or something?

Ted has struck a raw nerve. Sigfried's mood swings drastically; he bends down next to Ted.

SIGFRIED
Let's get our ABC's right, here, Theodore. Theodore, right?

TED
Ted's better.

SIGFRIED
Ted, okay . . . Are you saying my wife cheats on me?

TED
I didn't say that . . . I . . .

SIGFRIED
Oh, for Christ's sake, Theodore, this is about as intimate a situation as you can get, you, me, and Angela here. It's pretty cozy. To say nothing of how stupid an idea it is to lie to a man with a loaded gun without considering the possible response. I demand an apology!

The phone rings.

SIGFRIED
Don't move. I've got to take this.

Sigfried glances at it. Then to Angela. He picks up the phone.

SIGFRIED
(into phone)

What?
(pause)
We ain't got any needles here, kid. Just a big fucking gun.

He listens to the other line, says good-bye, and hangs up.

SIGFRIED
(to Ted)
Now, where was I? Oh yeah, I remember.

Sigfried kneels next to Ted and assumes a prayer position.

SIGFRIED
I want you to pray for forgiveness, Theodore.

Sigfried, hands clasped together, signals for Ted to do the same. The gun lies at his side. Ted considers a bold move, but thinks better of it. Sigfried's eyes pop open. He cuts a look to Ted, signaling him to assume the pose.

SIGFRIED
(continuing)
Now say after me, "I apologize . . ."

TED
I apologize . . .

SIGFRIED
For what?

Ted looks to Angela for help. She can only stare back with intense, wide-open eyes.

SIGFRIED
For fucking what?

TED
That I said you might have been unfaithful?

SIGFRIED

"That I said you might have been unfaithful?" Listen, Theodore, you're in church here . . . you're kneeling in front of
an altar. Truth . . . truth is all it hears. Say the following,
"I, Theodore, must humbly and sincerely apologize for saying that you fucked another man!"

*Ted repeats what Sigfried has told him. This appears to have a
calming effect on Sigfried, who gets up off the floor, turning his
face to Angela.*

SIGFRIED
(continuing)

Satisfied?

Angela nods.

SIGFRIED
(continuing)
Do you accept the fucking apology?

Naturally, Angela says nothing.

SIGFRIED
(continuing)
You always gotta get the last word, don't you? It's one way
with you, Angela, isn't it? I give and I give and I get nothing
back.

Sigfried turns back to Ted.

SIGFRIED
(continuing)
She just sits there waiting for me to jump through hoops. . . .

Angela attempts to speak through the gag. Both men wait with bated breath for a response. Sigfried's had enough.

SIGFRIED
(continuing)

Stupid me, for a second I thought you were going to say something . . . something like, "I'm sorry." HA! "I'm sorry." You're absolutely right, love cakes, I wouldn't want it that way. That's one thing you can say about Angela. She'll never do anything she doesn't want to do. If the feeling ain't there, she just isn't going to do it. There is nothing in this world as fucked as a woman who gives when she doesn't want to. Never let that happen to you, Theodore. It makes you feel very little indeed.

Ted beckons Sigfried.

TED

You mind if I . . . ?

SIGFRIED

Go ahead. Spit it out.

TED

I don't mean to upset you further, sir, but I think she was trying to say yes.

SIGFRIED

Are you condescending to me, Theodore?

TED

Absolutely not, I would never do that.

SIGFRIED

Why don't you just say it?

                        TED

Say what?

                     SIGFRIED

That you think I'm an idiot.

                        TED

I would never say that.

                     SIGFRIED

You think you're superior to me, don't ya, Theodore? You
don't think I notice there is a gag in the woman's mouth.

                        TED

Of course you do.

                     SIGFRIED

Naturally "of course." And do you know how I know that?

                        TED

How, sir?

                     SIGFRIED

Because I PUT THE GAG IN HER MOUTH! I'm gonna let
you in on a little secret about communication, Theodore.
It's all in the eyes . . .
                  (points the gun at Ted)
Him?
                  (turns the gun on himself)
Or me? Him or me? No one? Okay. Let's drag it out.

*Sigfried empties the last of the pills into his mouth, heaving the
empty bottle over his shoulder. He takes off, disappearing into the
bathroom.*

INT. ROOM 404

Ted finds himself alone with Angela. They lock eyes. Angela im-plores Ted to lean forward. Ted sizes up the situation: his chances of making it to the door are slim due to the fact that he would have to pass by the bathroom door. Ted paces back and forth in front of Angela, who struggles to get his attention. He whips around and they face off in what appears to be a game of cha-rades. Ted finally gets the point and cautiously removes the gag from Angela's mouth. Angela spits an old sock out.

TED

What!

ANGELA

We don't have time to play charades here, asshole! Untie me quick.

                    TED

Listen, lady, I don't know what in the hell is going on here,
but I'd appreciate it if you would explain to that nutcase
that he's making a big mistake.

                  ANGELA

Look, whether you like it or not, you're in the middle of a
situation here you can't just wish your way out of.

                    TED

But I've never seen you people before, we're complete
strangers.

                  ANGELA

Everyone starts out strangers, Ted, it's where we end up
that counts. Hurry up.

Ted wrestles with the idea of whether to untie Angela or not.

                    TED

I don't know if I can do this. It's too hard.

                  ANGELA

Life is hard, Ted. You ever stopped to consider how many
times you change your underwear in a lifetime?

On nervous impulse Ted begins the calculations.

                  ANGELA

I don't mean literally, you ignoramus.

                    TED

What?

ANGELA

Forget it, listen to me. There's a gun in my suitcase behind the bed, it's loaded . . .

TED

I'm not going to shoot anybody.

ANGELA

Fine. Get the gun and I'll shoot "anybody."

TED

And make me an accessory in the murder of your husband?

Ted collapses to his knees in front of Angela.

TED

That's not fair. It just isn't fair.

ANGELA

Get a fucking grip on yourself. First off, who says he's my husband? And second, we are a long way from fair here, fair is back in jolly old England eatin' crumpets and sipping on tea.

Ted collects himself.

TED

Tut. Tut. Tut. Not so fast. Well, maybe there are two sides to this thing.

ANGELA

There are two sides to a plate still you only eat off of one. Now GET THE GUN!

TED

So why's he got you tied up?

ANGELA

I'm a werewolf, Ted! Get the gun!

Ted is at a loss as to what to do. Angela turns on the charm.

ANGELA

Come on, Ted. Come over here just for a minute. You can do it. Come on, Ted. You look like a good guy.

Ted creeps toward her.

ANGELA

That's it, Teddy. You look so much more attractive when you're self-assured.

Sigfried suddenly comes to life. . . . He's heard from the bathroom belting out "Life is but a dream . . . she-boom, she-boom."

ANGELA
(She panics)

Quick, he's coming back. Put the gag back in, and remember the gun!

Ted hurries to replace the sock in her mouth.

TED

Nine thousand, three hundred and twenty-two times, to the best of my estimation.

INT. ROOM 404

Sigfried coughs, sending a chill up Ted's spine. Ted whips around to discover Sigfried leaning up against the door to the bathroom.

SIGFRIED

I was just beginning to think I could trust you, Theodore.
Silly me.

Ted's fingers are frozen over Angela's lips.

TED

I was just trying to help her breathe a little.

SIGFRIED

Don't let me stop you, Teddy. You don't mind me calling
you Teddy, do you?

TED

That's fine.

SIGFRIED

I used to have a little bunny rabbit named Teddy, it looked
real cute nibbling on Angela's ear. Only problem here is
you're no bunny rabbit, Theodore, and it really fuckin'
razzes me to picture you doin' it. But don't let me stop you,
Teddy . . . no need to play sneaky-poo.

Ted starts to back toward the door.

TED

Look, man, if this is some kind of Voodoo thing and you
want me to have sex with your wife, there is absolutely no
way.

SIGFRIED
(shouts at the top of his lungs)
I said, nibble, asshole! Now!

The directness of Sigfried's command, coupled with the SOUND of a trigger being cocked, forces Ted to approach Angela. Angela is a stunning beauty, and Ted being kind of a shy guy makes for an awkward situation. Ted leans forward. As he closes in, Angela's eyes close.

> TED
> (whispers)
>
> Sorry, lady.

Ted pulls up short of actually nibbling on Angela.

> SIGFRIED
>
> What's the matter, no whiz left in the cheese? I'm not cramping your style, am I?

> TED
>
> Look, I'm not playing this game anymore.

Sigfried yanks Ted backwards. He wraps his arms around him.

> SIGFRIED
>
> It's almost all over, Theodore, and soon you can go home to Mommy.

Ted struggles to free himself from Sigfried's powerful bear hug and blasts out the following monologue.

> TED
>
> My name is not Theodore it's TED, TED, TED, T . . . E . . . D. . . . TED. . . . NOT TEDDY, NOT THEODORE . . . TED. . . . Yes, my mother did me the service of naming me Theodore and I haven't a clue as to how you know that because everyone who knows that lives a long way away from here. Do you have any idea what it's

like to go to school where all the other kids' parents are in
jail doing time for crimes like grand larceny, aggravated
assault, burglary, and murder, and you get stuck with a
mother who names you Theodore and dressed you up in
little matching pink outfits with, get this, a little blue bow
fucking tie! Well, I'll tell you what happens. Pretty soon
Theodore becomes "Theo the Thumper," and when Theo
the Thumper gets old enough, he picks up his bags and
goes thousands of miles away where he can put the whole
bloody mess behind him. So, if you don't mind, shoot me
now, because no one is going to call me that again. My
name is Ted, okay? Got it? TED!

*Sigfried has followed the entire tirade in stunned silence. He takes
a step toward Ted and offers him his hand.*

>   SIGFRIED
> Sigfried.

>   TED
> What?

>   SIGFRIED
> My name is Sigfried.

>   TED
> Sigfried?

Sigfried cuts a "Something wrong with that?" look at Ted.

>   SIGFRIED
> Yah, Sigfried.

>   TED
> Nice to meet you, Sigfried.
>   *(Ted cautiously takes Sigfried's hand)*

SIGFRIED

Very impressive, Ted. "Theo the Thumper?" . . . Ouch. It's
a deal, kid. Ted it will be.

TED

Thanks.

*Sigfried holds on to Ted's hand. The soft sound of distant fireworks
pops in the background. Car horns and a muffled countdown sig-
nal that it's New Year's. Sigfried moves uncomfortably close to Ted
and from out of nowhere bolts forward, planting a wet kiss right
on Ted's mouth. Something snaps in Sigfried. He is either really
getting off on this or he is caught in the grips of a seizure. He
doubles back on the floor. Ted and Angela watch as he flops
around like a flounder with the cocked gun waving all over the
place. Ted wipes his mouth with his jacket sleeve while trying to
dodge the barrel of the gun.*

TED

You okay, mister? I'll get help!

*Sigfried manages to steady the gun and point it directly at Ted.
He signals for Ted to go to the bathroom.*

TED

(continuing)

That's the wrong door, sir.

*Sigfried grabs Ted by the leg and shoves the barrel of the gun into
his crotch. Sigfried pulls Ted's face close to his.*

SIGFRIED

Get me the nitro . . . it's in the bathroom cabinet. *Now!*

Ted rushes into the bathroom, leaving Sigfried a babbling mess behind.

CUT TO:

INT. BATHROOM—SAME TIME

Ted enters the bathroom, which appears shaken by an earthquake. Towels and wet clothes are all over the place. An evening gown is flushed halfway down the toilet and pills are everywhere. Sigfried is shouting from the other room to hurry. Ted checks the cabinet, searching for a bottle marked "Nitro." No luck. Ted spots a small window set above the toilet.

He figures this is the best chance he's got to make a break.

Ted goes for it. He manages to get his head and one arm through the window before he gets stuck. His legs dangle in the bathroom. Struggle as he may, he can only hit the toilet-bowl lever, which sends a loud FLUSH SOUND out through the apartment.

SIGFRIED (OS)
(shouting in the distance)
It's no time to take a leak, Teddy, I'm fucking dying here!

EXT. BATHROOM WINDOW—NIGHT

Outside the window, Ted's in another world. He's almost safe. It's a strange feeling, kind of like bathing in warm water in paradise, knowing a huge shark is ready to rip his ass off. He can see the flickering red glowing light from the witches' room from the floor below.

EXT. BATHROOM WINDOW AND BELOW—NIGHT

Ted sees Eva bopping naked past the window. He shouts her name out, to no avail. The MUSIC drowns out his voice and they ignore his calls for help. The blood rushes to his head. He lets himself hang there for a moment. He wonders how many other people have found themselves in positions like this before him. Probably every-one. Right next to his face, Ted recognizes a bloody hand print. It's not his blood.

EXT. BATHROOM WINDOW AND ABOVE—NIGHT

Ted hears a sound from above and twists himself around, spotting a young man (seen previously as the Yuppie Scumbag on the phone) leaning out of the window directly above him. After a quick moment of sizing him up, Ted gathers himself.

                    TED
  Hi . . .

No answer. Something's wrong with the guy, all the blood is drained from his face and he is mumbling something.

                    TED
  Listen, I'm stuck here in a situation that I can't even begin to explain, but would you be so kind as to get help. Could you call the police, please?

Silence.

                    TED
                 (continuing)
  You okay?

The young man manages to belt out the word "ice" just before hurling a mouthful of vomit toward Ted. It takes all Ted's strength to dodge the puke and pull himself back into the bathroom. He falls back on the floor.

He props himself up and checks for damage. He notices something odd . . . the room is silent. No Sigfried. He walks into the bedroom.

CUT TO:

INT. HOTEL BEDROOM—MOMENTS LATER

Ted looks around the still room. No one's there.

                    TED
  Sigfried?

He heads toward the door and, from out of the corner of his eye, he spots Sigfried's hairy leg. Sigfried has passed out on the floor. Angela's chair has been knocked on its side. Ted races over to help lift her back up. He pulls the gag from her mouth. Angela jumps all over him.

ANGELA

Where's the fucking nitro?

TED

I couldn't find it!

ANGELA

You took long enough. Untie me, for Christ's sake, you fucking upset him and he's dying.

Ted struggles to untie Angela.

TED

I thought you wanted to kill him.

ANGELA

You'd make a great cop, Theodore.

The knots are all over the place and a real bitch to untie.

TED

I can't handle this alone, I'd better get help.

Ted turns on a dime and runs smack into Sigfried, who's been taking in the whole conversation.

SIGFRIED

I tie a pretty good knot, don't I, Ted?

TED

Thank God you're okay . . .

SIGFRIED

Never felt better.

Angela hears Sigfried's voice from behind her back.

ANGELA

You bastard!

SIGFRIED

(to Angela)

Come on, honey, don't get mad. It was just a little test, and I'm glad I did it because now I'll know forever that you really do love me. Truly and deeply.

ANGELA

If the simple fact that I didn't want your bloated, dead body lying out on the floor is love, then no wonder we find ourselves as we are at this very fucking moment.

SIGFRIED

Oh, no. I heard you and there was genuine care in that voice. Can't be denied. Can it, Ted?

TED

I think you're right and, if you just keep this kind of open dialogue going, you'll go a long way to resolving this misunderstanding.

Ted edges his way toward the door.

TED
(continuing)

You'd be surprised what happens when people just listen to each other without succumbing to all that pain and anger.

ANGELA

You heard shit, monkey boy. Easy for you to say after you fuck another man's wife. You should at least have the guts to stand by your convictions.

Sigfried turns an icy eye on Ted, who has given up all hope of ever getting out of the room.

TED

That's a lie, Sigfried. I swear to God.

Angela continues her tirade.

ANGELA

When I think of all the times you were inside me promising
me a better life, it makes me want to puke.

Sigfried slowly raises his gun, pointing it directly at Ted's chest.

TED

Why are you doing this? What have I ever done to you
people?

ANGELA

What didn't you do, stick man? Unfortunately, you don't
have the balls to back up the actions of your huge cock.

The words hit Sigfried like bullets to the chest . . . his legs weaken.

SIGFRIED
(whimpering)

He's got a huge cock?

TED

She's lying again, mister. It's not that big.

SIGFRIED

Show it to me.

TED

Come on, man, she's lying. Can't you see she's fucking with
you?

ANGELA

Put it this way, God made up for what He did to Gumby
with Teddy here.

SIGFRIED

Show it to me.

ANGELA

Show him your cock, Theodore.

Sigfried runs over to Angela and kneels in front of her.

SIGFRIED

Stop talking about his cock, will you!

ANGELA

It's hard to stop talking about something so huge. I could
go on and on about his cock, bone, nob, bishop, wang,
thang, hotrod. Hump mobile, Oscar, dong, dagger, banana,
cucumber, salami. Sausage, kielbasa, schlong, dink, tool,
Big Ben, Mister Happy, prick, disk, pecker, peter, pee-pee,
wee-wee, weiner, pisser, pistol, joint, hose, horn, middle-
leg, third-leg, meat, stick, joy-stick, dip-stick.

*Angela is on a roll. She fires the words at Sigfried, hitting him
pointblank. He staggers. He pleads with her to stop, covering his
ears. Ted watches the man crumble.*

ANGELA

(continuing)

Junior, the little head, little guy, Rumple Foreskin, Tootsie
Roll. Snake, one-eyed monster, one-eyed wonder, shaft,
sword, meat whistle, skin flute, love muscle, Roto-Rooter,
instrument, banger, rammer, ramrod, cherrypicker, log,
pole.

*Sigfried tries jamming the sock back in her mouth to stop the flow;
she manages to give him a "fuck of a bite" in the process. Mean-
while, Ted figures this to be his moment to make a move and bolts
for the door, only to be tackled by Sigfried at the one-yard line.
After a struggle, the two men rest on the floor, catching their
breath in a relaxed embrace.*

SIGFRIED

Please, don't leave me. I'll call you Ted from now on.

TED

It's not me, mister, I swear.

SIGFRIED

Personally, I don't give a fuck, Ted, it's just I don't want to be alone right now. I'm feeling a little vulnerable.

Sigfried heaves the gun over his shoulder, grabs a half-empty bottle of Jack Daniel's, and passes it to Ted, who takes a hit.

SIGFRIED

(continuing)

No guns, okay? Just you and me, Ted. You know my father used to say that forgiveness is the only thing that evil can't sink its teeth into.

TED

That's beautiful.

SIGFRIED

Kind of nice down here on the floor, isn't it, Ted?

TED

Yes, actually.

SIGFRIED

Things take on a whole new perspective. . . . You'd like my trust, wouldn't you, Ted?

TED

Yes I would.

SIGFRIED

I just got one thing to ask you and I'll let you go.

TED

Okay. Okay.

SIGFRIED

Tell me straight now.

TED

What?

SIGFRIED

What was it like?

TED

What was what like?

SIGFRIED

You know, you and her.

TED

Oh, for fuck sake, Sigfried, what do you want me to say?

SIGFRIED

Either way you're fucked, right? You ever gonna see her again, Theodore?

TED

If I ever saw her again, I'd run the other way.

SIGFRIED

Promise?

TED

I promise.

Sigfried releases Ted and stands up.

SIGFRIED

You're lying, but I can respect that, Ted. If you told me, it
would no longer be a secret, and secrets have a power, kid.
You open that box and they disappear forever. A bad secret
will rip you apart, but the good ones are all you got. In the
end, when all the people you knew are dead and gone, all
you'll have left are your secrets. And when you die, the box
is open and it all just blows away—dust to dust—all the
anger, jealousy, desire, and love just blow away.

Sigfried throws his hand out to help Ted up.

SIGFRIED
(continuing)
So you know what I say, let's call it a truce, kiddo.

*Sigfried takes Ted by the hand and leads him to an open window.
Ted is overcome by the sweetness in Sigfried's voice and follows
him to the window willingly. The two men look out into the dark
Los Angeles night.*

SIGFRIED
(continuing)
I'm a man of love, Theodore. Love is all I live for.

TED

I can see that.

SIGFRIED

Maybe to a fault.

TED

Don't beat yourself up over it.

SIGFRIED

That's nice of you to say, Ted, but I probably should make
a clean break of it, cut her loose and get my own place. I
just can't imagine living without her. Do you think I should
seek professional help?

TED

It's not for everyone, but maybe in your case it could help.

SIGFRIED

You ever been out on the ocean at night?

Ted shakes his head.

SIGFRIED
(continuing)
I have . . . scary as a motherfucker, all that darkness around
you. It's like a big black carpet rolled out as far as the eye
can see. Sometimes, if you're lucky, you'll see a light. It
could be as small as a little spark, but it will cut a path
straight through all that blackness, straight to you. It could
be another boat, or some distant fire on an island, but that
light will shed a shining path of diamonds cutting through
mile after mile of darkness to lie at your feet. That's love,
Ted, it's like a path of light in an ocean of darkness.

*Ted and Sigfried stare out of the window in peace, transfixed by
the glimmering lights of the city. A loud SHOT rings out, shatter-
ing the still moment. The two men spin around. Angela stands
there with a smoking gun hanging at her side. Sigfried drops to
his knees. Ted checks him out, no blood. Angela has fired the gun
into the floor below. Ted looks up at Angela. Angela opens the
chamber of the pistol and hands the bullets to Ted.*

ANGELA
(to Ted)
You'd better go check to see if I killed anybody downstairs.

Sigfried is bent over, silently weeping on the floor.

TED
You people gonna be okay?

Angela sits next to Sigfried and gently strokes his back.

ANGELA
We're fine, Ted.

Ted points to a tray with half-eaten food on it.

TED
Would you like me to . . . ?

ANGELA
Another time, Ted.

Ted slowly walks toward the door and takes one last look at the strange couple at rest in the corner of the room before closing the door behind him.

CUT TO:

INT. HALLWAY—MOMENTS LATER

Ted walks down the hallway, lost in thought. An energetic Young Guy with a bouquet of flowers plows into him.

YOUNG GUY
Happy New Year, buddy.

TED
Happy New Year.

YOUNG GUY
I was just in room 404, what a party! You know where room 409 is at?

TED
Beats me. It's somewhere around here.

The guy takes off in the direction Ted's walking from. Ted suddenly realizes who this guy is and whips around, shouting to the Young Guy.

TED
(continuing)
Hey, what's your name?

The door SLAMS on room 409.

FADE OUT

FADE TO BLACK

STORY TITLE CARD:

room 716

■

the
misbehavers

robert
rodriguez

■

FADE UP

THE FRONT DESK SUPER: *10:30* P.M.

Ted is relaxing at the front desk. He breathes slowly. He finally has one moment's peace after an already long night. He even has a chance to straighten his tie.

The phone RINGS.

                              TED
       Front desk?

CUT TO:

ROOM 716.

CLOSE-UP of a cigarette hanging out of a Man's mouth as he speaks into the telephone.

MAN
Bottle of Moët et Chandon. Fast.

Man hangs up the phone and stubs out his cigarette into an already overstuffed ashtray by the bed. Man turns around to face the camera. He is a dark and handsome Latin male in his mid-30s. Dangerous. Impatient.

He walks toward the camera as he continues straightening his tie.

He stops at the door of the bathroom and watches his Wife and two kids get ready for the party. Wife seems to be a beautiful woman in her mid-30s. The children are Sarah, nine, and Juancho, six.

Man strikes up another cigarette and finishes his tie.

He watches his Wife comb Juancho's hair down and to the side like an idiot.

Not being able to stand it any more, Man tears Juancho away from his Wife and snatches the comb.

MAN
Give me that . . .

Man begins to slick Juancho's hair back.

MAN
There . . . see? You look cool with your hair up like this. Like me. . . .

Juancho is smiling now. He's happy he's going to look like his dad.

MAN

Not down and to the side, all stupid like your mom likes to comb it.

Juancho looks over at Sarah, who is going through the tortuous ritual of having her mother brush the tangles out of her long, unmanageable hair.

Wife seems to be taking out her aggressions on the tangled mess.

Man is starting to have problems of his own with Juancho's hair. Juancho's hair is thinner than Man's, so it won't stay up.

Man puts down his cigarette in order to get a better handle on it. We see the frustration growing in his face.

Juancho picks up the cigarette and pretends he's smoking too, just like his dad.

Man tears the cigarette away from Juancho and smokes it down

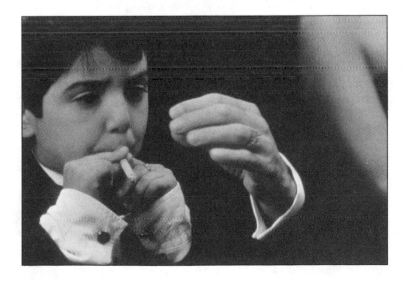

*to the filter. He looks at his own cool hair, and then down at
Juancho's, which won't stay up.*

Man flicks the cigarette butt into the toilet in frustration.

MAN

You've got your mother's hair.

In anger, Man starts messing up Juancho's hair.

MAN

I can't do anything with it.

*Furious, Man simply swipes Juancho's hair back down and to the
side, the way Wife had it before. Juancho looks like an idiot again.*

MAN

There. Go.

Juancho slouches past everyone as he exits the bathroom.

Sarah watches him leave as her own hair is finished.

WIFE
(putting a plastic clip in Sarah's hair)

There. Go.

Sarah exits.

*Wife then finishes her own gorgeous hair. Man lights up a new
cigarette.*

WIFE
(mocking)

So, are we gonna have fun tonight?

Man blows smoke in Wife's face as he walks out of the bathroom.

> WIFE
> I didn't think so.

Sarah has joined Juancho in watching television.

Man watches the children watch TV. We can see the wheels turning in Man's head.

He turns back to the bathroom.

He watches Wife now. Wheels turning. Practically burning rubber.

> MAN
> Hey.

Wife puts the lipstick down and turns to her husband. She is beautiful.

> MAN
> *(shrugs)*
> Let's just leave the kids here.

Wife glances out at the children, eyes glued to the tube.

> WIFE
> Here in the room? By themselves?

> MAN
> No . . . with the television.

Wife thinks about it for a second. She shrugs a "sure."

> MAN
> You want to have fun tonight, don't you?

                    WIFE
Yes.

                    MAN
They'll be fine.

*He kisses Wife's face and exits the bathroom. She covers the wet
spot with more cake makeup.*

                    MAN
Hey.

The children turn to face him.

                    MAN
You guys are going to stay here and watch TV.

The children look at each other.

                    MAN
I want you to be in bed asleep before twelve. Your mother
and I will be back later on.

Wife goes straight for the door.

                              MAN
      Okay?

He blows one kiss. One for both of them.

As Man and his Wife walk out the door, Man turns back to the children. . . .

                              MAN
      Don't misbehave.

He closes the door.

Sarah stands in the middle of the room. She's looking at the door Man and Wife just disappeared through. Stunned.

Her dress looks frilly and beautifully uncomfortable. She touches the edges of the fabric.

                            SARAH
      Why did we have to get all dressed up if we weren't going
      with them?

      CUT TO:

INT. HALLWAY

Man and wife are walking down the hall.

Man stops in his tracks. Wife stops too, and looks at Man. They wait.

      CUT TO:

ROOM 716

Juancho shuts off the television. He drops the remote to the floor. His attention is on the fireworks outside. He leaps to the window and begins unlatching it.

SARAH

What are you doing?

JUANCHO

Escaping. Stinks in here, anyway.

Man bursts through the door of the hotel room and stands in the doorway, glaring at the mischievous Juancho.

Juancho bangs his head on the window trying to get back inside. He leaps to the floor and tries to turn on the TV with the remote.

MAN
(stern)

What did I say?

Juancho turns to Man as if he'd been sitting there watching television the whole time.

MAN

Behave.

JUANCHO

Yes, Papa.

Ted appears at the door with Man's champagne.

TED

The champagne you ordered, sir.

MAN

No time for this. Leave it on ice.

Ted proceeds to place the champagne in the room.

WIFE

But I want some now. . . .

Ted is torn. Man pushes him into the room.

MAN

There'll be plenty for you at the party, baby, you can bomb yourself all you want at the party.

WIFE

What a waste.

Ted places the bucket near the bed. After setting up the bottle, he turns to leave, but now Man closes the door, trapping Ted inside with them.

MAN
(to Ted)

Hey.

Ted looks around, bewildered. Now what?

Man is reaching into his coat pocket.

MAN

You want five hundred bucks?

TED

Sure!

Man hesitates a moment, then pulls out his wallet. That was too easy.

                    MAN
How about three?

                    TED
Three hundred?

                    MAN
Yeah.

                    TED
Three's good.

                    MAN
My children are staying here tonight watching TV. I want
you to check up on them every thirty minutes.

                    TED
Check up on 'em?

                    MAN
Make sure they're all right, make sure they're fed, make
sure they go to bed.

                    TED
We can call out and hire a baby-sitter.

                    MAN
I don't trust baby-sitters. My children are safer alone than
with some fucked-up pedophile baby-sitter I don't know
from the man in the fucking moon.

WIFE
What about him? What makes you think you can trust him?

Man grabs Ted's face and tilts it toward Wife.

MAN
Tell me that's not a face you can trust.

Man lets go of Ted's face. He feels his jaw. It's still there.

TED
Look, sir, I'd like to help you out, but I really can't. I'm all alone here tonight.

Man whips out his wallet and counts out money in Ted's face.

MAN
One hundred . . . two hundred . . . three hundred. . . .

TED
I thought you said five hundred.

Man glares at Ted.

MAN
I said three hundred.

Ted doesn't back down.

TED
No, you distinctly said five hundred.

The angrier Man gets, the quieter he talks.

> MAN

You calling me a liar?

Ted, while not backing down, massages the situation.

> TED

No, I'm not saying you're lying. I'm saying you accidentally forgot that what you first said was five hundred.

Man has never been challenged like this by a fuckin' bellboy.

> MAN

I don't do anything accidentally, jerk. I might've first said five hundred, but what I last said was three hundred, and what you say last is what counts.

Ted not only doesn't back down, but psychologically pokes his finger in the scary Man's chest.

> TED

Well then, if you say five hundred one last time, we got a deal.

Man's eyes narrow. He physically pokes his finger in Ted's chest.

> MAN

You fuckin' with me, Pendejo?

Now Ted takes a step backwards.

> TED

No, not at all. It's New Year's Eve and I'm here alone. If there was somebody else here, no problem, but I'm by myself. And looking after your kids is a pain in the ass I don't need—

                              MAN
You callin' my kids a pain in the ass?

                              TED
—No, they're not a pain in the ass, it's the situation that's
a pain in the ass.

Man drops the tenseness.

                              MAN
No, you were right the first time. You win, tough guy, five
hundred.

*Man respects Ted for not backing down, but not insulting him
either. A skill Man never learned. Wife shoots a look at the children.*

                             WIFE
                          (disgusted)
You kids are getting expensive.

Juancho turns back to the TV.

Sarah stares down Wife.

                              MAN
                     (looking at name tag)
What's your name? Ted?

CLOSE-UP *of name tag.*

                              TED
Yeah. It's Ted.

Man tears off Ted's name tag and throws it to the children.

MAN
(to the children)
His name is Ted. If you need anything, dial 0 and ask for
Ted.

*Sarah catches the name tag and reads the name on it: "TED—
BELLHOP."*

*Sarah looks up at Ted. She clips the pin to her dress and smiles
shyly at him.*

*Man puts the money in Ted's pocket and then grabs his ear, pull-
ing him close.*

MAN
(deadly whisper)
If something happens to my children, I wouldn't want to be
you.

WIFE
Make sure they're in bed before midnight.

TED
(thinking)
Before midnight? Then should I wake them up for the
countdown to the New Year?

Wife looks disgusted.

WIFE
No . . .

As Man and Wife exit, he turns to the kids and says:

MAN

Don't misbehave.

Man closes the door.

INT. HALLWAY

Man and Wife book it down the hall before Ted can change his mind.

ROOM 716

Ted is standing facing the door the Man and Wife just disappeared through. He turns around slowly to face the children.

His eyes are wide. His face is quiet. Stern.

The children are staring at him.

TED

Okay. These are the rules. Don't break the rules and I won't break your necks.

The kids look at each other.

TED
(smiling)

I always wanted to say that. Someone said that to me when I was a kid.

Sarah laughs at his joke.

TED

Except they weren't joking. I am.

Ted goes to the door.

TED

The rules are simple. Don't do anything you wouldn't do if your parents were here. If there's an emergency, call me on the phone, like your dad said.

SARAH

That's not what he said.

Ted's surprised by a challenge this early in the game.

SARAH

He said to call if we need anything.

TED

Well, I've got a lot of work to do and I can't have you calling me every time you want a drink of water, so please limit your calls to emergencies only.

SARAH

We paid you five hundred dollars. We'll call you if we need anything. You don't want to upset my dad.

TED

Okay. Please. Try to call only when necessary. Watch TV, and if you're good, I'll bring up some milk and cookies. Bye.

Ted leaves.

CUT TO:

INT. HALLWAY

Ted walks briskly down the hall, counting his money the whole way.

CUT TO:

INT. ROOM 716

Juancho takes off his socks and shoes and throws them onto the floor. Sarah looks at the discarded shoes and socks.

CLOSE ON *the shoes and socks.*

Sarah looks over at Juancho's bare feet. Her nose twitches.

SARAH
Your feet stink.

Juancho smells his feet.

JUANCHO
They don't stink.

Sarah throws his shoes and socks behind her. They land on the bed.

Juancho is flipping channels and finds an interesting show.

JUANCHO
Check it out. T & A.

Sarah realizes he found a Nudie station.

SARAH

Change it. You're not supposed to watch this.

JUANCHO

We're supposed to watch TV.

SARAH

Not this kind of TV. Change it.

Juancho rolls up in a ball, the remote tucked in some recess of his stomach.

Sarah hits him, then goes to the phone. She punches 0, sits on the bed, and checks the name on the name tag pinned to her shirt.

CUT TO:

FRONT DESK

Ted walks up to the front desk just as the phone rings.

TED

Front desk.

INT. ROOM 716

Sarah is taking off her white winter tights.

SARAH

Ted? Hi. It's me, Sarah. You're our sitter for tonight.

TED

Oh, Jesus, what did I tell you? I said if you don't bother me, you'll get milk and cookies. Now, do you want them or do you not?

SARAH

I want you to turn off the Nudie station in our room.

Ted checks the computer.

TED
(reading stats on room 716)
I can't turn on an adult station without permission from your parents.

SARAH

No.
(struggling with winter tights)
Not turn it on, turn it off. It's already on.

TED

That's not what the machine tells me.

SARAH

Well, stop listening to the machine and listen to me. There's naked ladies dancing on my TV and I want 'em off.

TED

If you're good, you'll get milk and cookies, so leave me alone, please. I'll be up later to put you both to sleep.

He hangs up.

ROOM 716

Angry, Sarah slams down the phone. She has an unusually adult temper. We know where she gets it from. She looks up and sees that the nudies are still in full force.

SARAH

Change the channel, now!

Juancho turns around. He has a face like someone just laid a fart in his nose.

JUANCHO

Man, you're the one with the stinky feet!

Sarah smells her feet. Twice.

SARAH

They don't stink.

JUANCHO

Yeah, they do.

SARAH

Here, smell for yourself.

She sticks her foot out for Juancho to smell. He's reluctant. Fearful.

SARAH

Go ahead.

He slowly, very slowly . . . climbs onto the bed and lowers his head to her foot. Very slowly.

Sarah waits until he's close enough to her foot before she kicks him in the face, sending him somersaulting off the bed and crashing to the floor.

She grabs the remote control he left behind and changes the channel to a cartoon.

Juancho gets up and realizes his defeat. He decides to wander about. Looking for something to do. . . .

Sarah tries to ignore him as he stalks the room. It's only a matter of time before he finds mischief.

Juancho sees the champagne bucket and Bingo!, he goes for the bottle.

JUANCHO
(holding up the bottle)
Hey, get a bottle opener!

Sarah opens her mouth, as if about to tell him to leave the champagne alone. She stops herself when she realizes she wants some champagne too.

She quickly scrambles about for a bottle opener while Juancho unwraps the bottle top.

Sarah opens the dresser drawer with such force that a few hidden contents long forgotten in the back of the drawer slide forward.

Some coins, a paperclip, and a hypodermic needle. She looks down at the needle that lays beside the Gideon Bible and casually picks the phone back up and punches 0. The phone rings.

FRONT DESK

Ted, bucket of ice in his hand, gets ready to go to room 404. As he crosses the desk, the phone rings. He looks at the board and sees room 716's light blinking. He sighs in exasperation.

INT. ROOM 716

Sarah sees Juancho shaking the champagne bottle violently.

SARAH

Don't shake it!

(into phone)

Ted? Hi. It's me. Sarah.

TED

Yeah. Who died? No one? Then don't call me.

SARAH

I just thought I'd tell you that your cleaning ladies are doing
a bum job. There's all kinds of leftover stuff around here.

*Sarah picks up the needle and rolls it over in her hand several
times.*

SARAH

Needles and things. We're not supposed to have needles
here, are we? I mean, they don't come with the room, do
they? Send someone up here to clean this place up right.

The champagne bottle explodes all over Juancho. He looks surprised.

SARAH
(to Juancho)
I TOLD YOU NOT TO SHAKE IT!
(to Ted)

I gotta go. My brother just exploded the champagne all over the room. Oh, and bring us a couple of toothbrushes. There's a card in the bathroom that says you'll bring free toothbrushes if we ask for them.

She hangs up.

A frustrated Ted hangs up the phone. He walks briskly to the elevator.

Sarah and Juancho are pouring themselves champagne. They turn up the television and drink. Juancho shudders at the taste, but tries to drink as much as Sarah.

Sarah clearly doesn't like it, but tries to pretend like she does.

Sarah picks up an instruction card near the phone to see how to make room-to-room calls.

SARAH

I'm calling another room, give me three numbers.

JUANCHO

4-0-9.

Sarah punches in the room number. The phone rings.

She holds the needle up to the light to examine it.

SARAH
Hello? Hi. You don't know me, and I don't know you, but
. . . do you have any needles? We've got needles here and
I was wondering if they come with the room or not. Don't
have any? Thanks. Just checking.

She hangs up.

*Juancho puts down his champagne glass and searches his father's
coat pocket. He finds a pack of cigarettes and takes one out. He
puts it in his mouth and pretends to smoke.*

*Sarah checks out the hypodermic needle carefully. She has an
idea.*

MONTAGE:

In the bathroom, Sarah seeks out her mother's lipstick.

ROOM 716

*Sarah stands atop the chest of drawers and uses the lipstick to
draw a bull's-eye on one of the hotel art paintings. She writes
numbers next to each circle representing points.*

*Juancho is standing at the foot of the bed, cigarette hanging out
of his mouth, as he practices his dart-throwing technique.*

SARAH
(pointing out the rules)
The center is the bull's eye, 100 points, this one's 10
points, this one's 20 points.

*WHACK! The needle lands an inch from her face in the 20-point
slot.*

SARAH
Hey, wait a minute. Let me get out of the way!

*Sarah, a little tipsy now, grabs the needle and staggers to the bed.
She hears the key in the doorway and throws the needle into the
curtain to hide it.*

*Ted enters the room, somewhat disheveled from his encounter with
Sigfried. He has a tray and a new bottle of champagne.*

*He puts the champagne bottle into the empty bucket. He spots the
original bottle lying on the floor half empty and dripping into the
carpet.*

TED
I brought you some milk and cookies. If you want some you
have to eat them now, because you're going to sleep.

SARAH
We're going to sleep now?

TED
Your parents said put you to bed before midnight. Well, it's
before midnight. Maybe that way you'll leave me alone.

SARAH
Those aren't milk and cookies.

TED

We were out of cookies, so I brought you milk and Saltines. Don't complain! Now hurry up and eat. You're going to bed right now.

Juancho bites into a Saltine. Sarah simply examines one.

JUANCHO

These are old.

SARAH

They're stale.

TED
(impatient)
Dip 'em in the milk! The milk will make them soft.

Sarah gives up and throws the cracker back onto the tray. She's a little drunk.

Ted picks up the ruined champagne bottle.

Juancho dips his crackers and eats them. He makes a face and drops a soggy cracker onto the tray.

TED

No crackers? Okay, fine. Sleepy time. Now, I don't want you guys wandering around, so if you need to go to the restroom, *go now.*

They go to the bathroom. Ted sits on the bed. Waits.

He sees the painting on the wall but can't figure out what's different about it. The red lipstick blends right into the aesthetic value of the painting.

Ted smells something funny. He looks down and sees the socks on the bed. He grabs a fork from the tray and uses it to throw the socks across the room.

The kids come back out.

JUANCHO

What about our pajamas?

TED

You wanna look nice in case there's an earthquake, don'tcha?

The children nod.

TED

Okay. Then stay in those clothes.

The kids lie on the bed.

Sarah notices a jar of Mentholatum ointment on the dinner tray.

SARAH

What's that?

TED

Oh, this is just some Mentholatum ointment. Come on, under the covers. Close your eyes and I'll tell you a story.

The children close their eyes. Ted opens the jar of the ointment and sniffs it. Strong stuff by the look on his face.

TED

Your dad says he doesn't trust baby-sitters. I don't blame him. You know what my baby-sitter did to me once?

(confiding)
I never told my parents, either.

The children lie in the bed, eyes closed, listening intently.

Ted dips his fingers in the jar of vaporous ointment.

TED

I hated going to sleep. You know, it's nighttime and you
wanna run around and act crazy. So what my baby-sitter
did to make sure I'd go to sleep and not be tempted to get
up, was, she'd take some of this vapor rub stuff . . . Can
you smell this?

Eyes closed, the kids inhale. They smell the ointment and nod yes.

TED

Well, she'd just dab a little of this over each eyelid, so that
I would be sure and keep my eyes closed all night.

Ted is spreading the ointment over their eyelids as he says this.

TED

There. Now you've got some, too! Don't open your eyes or
it'll burrrn, burn, burn. The smell helps clear your sinuses
too, so it's doing double duty.

JUANCHO

What happens when it's morning?

TED

If you keep your eyes closed all night, it will wear off by
morning. But DON'T OPEN YOUR EYES BEFORE
THAT. . . .

                                SARAH
            Did you ever open your eyes?

Extreme CLOSE-UP *on Ted's eyes.*

                                 TED
                Yes . . . I did.

The children are quiet.

                                 TED
            And now look at me.

                              CHILDREN
                             (in unison)
                We can't.

                                 TED
            Good. You'll do just fine. Sleep well and I won't tell your
            parents about the champagne.

Ted leaves.

CUT TO:

AFTER A MOMENT OF DARKNESS

*After a moment of darkness, the night is disturbed by the loud
crashing of fireworks outside the window.*

*Sarah sits up, eyes closed. Her face feels the warmth coming from
the window and she tilts her head toward it.*

The light of the fireworks dances its reflections off her face.

She inhales deeply . . . then makes a sour face. She goes for the bathroom, arms outstretched like a blind girl. She gets to the bathroom, turns on the light, and searches for the sink.

She begins to wash the ointment off her eyes very carefully. She dries her eyes thoroughly and opens them . . . checks them in the mirror. A little red, but otherwise fine.

She goes back into the bedroom, turns on the television and grabs the new champagne bottle. She shakes it violently.

Juancho wakes. He turns his head to her. His eyes are still closed.

JUANCHO

Are you watching TV?

The champagne bottle explodes. She pours herself a glass.

SARAH

Yep. If you wanna watch too, you have to go wash your face.

Juancho gets up smiling and tries to run to the bathroom. He slams into the wall, hard.

SARAH

Be careful . . .

Juancho walks into the bathroom a little slower, more cautious.

Sarah pours herself another glass. She downs the glass and shudders.

She smells the bad smell again. Only now she really smells it.

She smells her feet. Nothing. She smells the champagne. Nothing.

Juancho enters the room and sits on the bed. Sarah grabs his foot and smells it. She drops his foot.

Juancho stares blankly at her.

Sarah looks down at the mattress. She smells the mattress.

Juancho looks at her as if she's drunk.

Sarah leaps off the bed and turns on the room lights. She takes a huge swig from the champagne bottle, then stalks toward the mattress.

Juancho leaps off the bed as well and stands back.

Sarah pulls the mattress off of the bedsprings enough to see what is underneath it.

Juancho screams. Sarah is too stunned to scream. Stuffed into the bedsprings is a woman's dead and beaten corpse.

CUT TO:
CLOSE ON

Ted's phone ringing.

Ted looks at the phone as if pondering whether or not to answer it. He taps his fingers. Finally he answers the phone.

ROOM 716

SARAH
Ted!

TED

What do you want now, for Christ's sake! Who died?

SARAH

(near tears)

I don't know, but she's in my bed!

TED

What?

SARAH

There's a dead body in my bed!

TED

That's just your brother! Sound asleep.

SARAH

No, there's a woman's dead body inside the bed, in the mattress!

TED

You saw the body?

SARAH

Yes!

TED

Impossible. You've got ointment on your eyes! You can't see shit. Now go to sleep!

Ted hangs up the phone.

Sarah redials.

Ted answers.

TED

Godammit, go to sleep!

SARAH

(crying now)

I washed it off . . .

TED

You washed off the ointment?

SARAH

(pissed, drunk)

Yeah, didn't you ever think to do that?

Ted is quiet on the line. Thinking.

Juancho lights up a cigarette for real and takes nervous puffs.

Sarah carries the phone over to Juancho and snatches the cigarette away from him. She stuffs it in her own mouth and nervously takes a long drag on it.

SARAH

(through cigarette)

You never tried it, did you? Then you agree that I'm smarter than you . . .

TED

All right. Now you listen to me . . .

SARAH

Get your ass up here and call the police, because there's a dead body in my bed and it smells like shit and it looks even worse, and if you don't help us, my dad is gonna lay you down right next to her, I swear to fucking God!

She drinks from her champagne bottle. She's pulling the mattress back over the corpse again.

JUANCHO

Go, sis.

She's drunk all right.

TED
(incensed)
I'm coming up and if there isn't a dead body by the time I get there, I'll make one myself. You!

FRONT DESK

Ted slams down the phone.

As he walks away from the counter, he spots the children's parents driving up to the valet out front.

TED

Oh shit!

Ted breaks into a sprint and dives into a closing elevator.

CUT TO:

ROOM 716

Sarah continues to cover the body with the mattress.

ELEVATOR

Close on Ted's face as the elevator car races up seven floors.

LOBBY

The Man is carrying his drunk Wife through the lobby. Not happy.

ROOM 716

Ted bursts into the room. He sees the disarray.

Ted pushes the champagne out of Sarah's hand, spilling it onto the floor.

> TED
> What the fuck is going on!

He sees Juancho with the cigarette hanging out of his mouth and rips it away from him. The butt goes flying onto the carpet near the spreading champagne spill.

> TED
> Your parents are on their way up and I'm not taking respon-
> sibility for this mess!

> SARAH
> Check under the mattress!

> TED
> For what?

SARAH
(crying)
For the body, can't you smell it?

TED

It's your feet!

Sarah grabs the mattress and pulls it off herself.

Ted sees the rotting corpse.

Vomit spews out of Ted's mouth.

TED
(gargles through vomit-spewing lips)
Jesus fucking Christ! What the fuck is this!

He tears at the phone.

TED
(into the phone)
Police, it's an emergency!
(pause)
Hello, Police, this is the Mon Signor Hotel, get someone up
here right fucking now, there's a DEAD WHORE stuffed
under the mattress!

Tears well in Sarah's eyes as she looks at the body.

SARAH

Don't call her that . . .

TED
(into the phone)
I'm dead fucking serious, there's a dead fucking Whore
stuffed in the bedsprings of the fucking bed!

                            SARAH
  Stop calling her that!!

*Sarah grabs the hypodermic needle from under the curtain and
stabs it into Ted's leg.*

                             TED
      FUCK!!

*Sarah steps back, almost tripping over the champagne bottle. She
picks up the bottle and holds it up defensively in case Ted tries to
retaliate. Ted spins around, now noticing the needle sticking out
of his leg.*

                             TED
      Jesus!!

Juancho lights up another cigarette.

*The champagne spill has spread to the fallen cigarette butt. The
carpet bursts into flames around the spill.*

CUT OUTSIDE TO:

EXT. ROOM 716

CLOSE ON *a key going into the keyhole outside.*

BACK TO:

ROOM 716

Ted tries to pull the syringe out of his leg, but yanking it makes it break in two, the plunger in his hand and the needle still stuck in his leg.

Ted staggers and grabs hold of the dead woman's foot for support as he steps on the remote control, flipping the TV on to the Nudie channel, just as . . .

Man opens the door.

Man stands at the door, drunk Wife unconscious on one arm, the door knob in the other hand. He's looking mean.

Man's POV: focused on the dead woman in the bedsprings. We pan up the dead woman's leg to find Ted holding her foot. We pan down Ted's leg to find the hypodermic needle jutting out . . . then pan over to the other hand holding the broken syringe plunger.

We pan over to the Nudie channel, then down to the fire blazing behind the children. Pan up to the dripping champagne bottle in Sarah's hand, then over to the cigarette hanging out of Juancho's mouth. Juancho tosses his cigarette out of his mouth to an area behind him. Another blaze starts immediately.

Man drops his Wife to the floor.

In the WIDE SHOT of Ted and the children, we see that the fire-works are bursting big and bright outside the window behind them. Almost as bright as the flames eating through the room.

Man simply glares at Ted. Finally Man speaks . . .

                    MAN
    Did they misbehave?

Ted stares blankly at Man (the camera) as the sprinklers burst on . . . drenching the room as the picture

FADES TO BLACK

MIRROR
Point
of
View

JUANCHO
&
MAN

OVER
SHOULDER
INTO
MIRROR

SAME
w/
SARA
&
WIFE

© 1994
ROBERT
RODRIGUEZ

STEADICAM
BACK
WITH
JUANCHO
TO
FRAMED
FOOT IN
FOREGROUND

COVER
KICK

LOW WIDE
ANGLE
AS
JUANCHO
FLIES
OFF
BED.

SARA
TESTS
THE
SHARPNESS
OF THE
NEEDLE

THUNK!

SHE STABS
IT INTO
THE BED
AS SHE
GOES TO
BATHROOM

JUANCHO
EYES
THE
NEEDLE

©1994
Robert
Rodriguez

JUANCHO
THROWS
NEEDLE

SPECIAL
EFFECT
SHOT

JUANCHO
SHRUGS

SARA
PUSHES
MATTRESS
OFF

JUANCHO
SCREAMS...

...AT THE
ROTTING
CORPSE

JUANCHO
LIGHTS
UP

SARA
SCREAMS
AT TED

"STOP CALLING HER THAT!"

SARA W/ NEEDLE

STAB

TED HOPS AROUND ROOM W/ NEEDLE IN LEG

©1994 ROBERT ROSKIND

JUANCHO
THROWS
CIGARETTE,
STARTS FIRE

HUGE
BLAZE

LAST SHOT,
MAN'S P.O.V.
FIRE, Needle,
Cig, Bottle,
&
FIREWORKS

ROBERT
RODRIGUEZ
© 11-94 FOUR
ROOMS

four rooms

FADE UP ON

INT. HOTEL LOBBY—NIGHT

SUPER: ONE MINUTE AFTER ROBERT'S STORY. TWENTY
MINUTES BEFORE DAWN.

*The elevator rides down to the lobby. The doors open and a wet,
disheveled, and frantic Ted steps out.*

*He staggers across the lobby to the reception desk. He grabs the
phone.*

INT. BETTY'S APT—ALMOST DAWN

*The wild New Year's Eve party is winding down. Some Guests are
passed out, some are asleep, some are making out, two guys are
playing Nintendo, a Girl watches them. The phone RINGS. The
Girl, who wears a "Guinness Stout" T-shirt, answers the phone.*

> GUINNESS GIRL
> Happy New Year!

BACK TO TED: BACK AND FORTH

> TED
> Let me speak to Betty.

GUINNESS GIRL

Party's over, she probably went home.

TED

She lives there.

GUINNESS GIRL

Oh, well, I haven't seen 'em in a while.

TED

Do you even know who I'm talking about?

GUINNESS GIRL

Yeah . . . yeah . . . yeah . . . I know 'em, I know Eddy.

TED

Betty, not Eddy.

GUINNESS GIRL

Yeah . . . Yeah . . . I know Betty too . . . Tall . . .

TED

No, not particularly. She's got curly red hair.

GUINNESS GIRL

No, no, no, no, no, I know, I know. Japanese girl.

TED

She's not Japanese! I just said she had red hair.

GUINNESS GIRL

Yeah . . . yeah . . . yeah . . . I know her.

TED

Well, then get her on the phone, it's an emergency.

GUINNESS GIRL

Who—who should I say's calling?

TED

Tell 'em Teddy from work's on the phone, and it's a major fuckin' emergency.

GUINNESS GIRL

Gotcha, Betty from work.

TED

Not Betty from work, I'm calling Betty! I'm Teddy. Just say Ted.

GUINNESS GIRL

Hi, Ted, I'm Margaret. You sound down. Has this not been the happiest of New Year's?

TED
(resigning himself to talking with Margaret)
No Margaret, this hasn't been my best New Year. This year's starting off pretty badly.

MARGARET

Awww, how come?

TED

Well, Betty—the chick whose house you're at, even though you don't know her—leaves me here all by myself on New Year's Eve. And first thing right off the bat, I'm fucked by a coven of witches.

MARGARET

An oven full of witches fucked you? Is that like at the circus when they stick all those clowns in an itty-bitty car?

TED

A *coven*. A *coven* of witches. Well, one witch in particular.

MARGARET

Was she an old hag with a mole, with hair growing out of it?

TED

No-no-no, she was . . . quite beautiful.

Margaret thinks for a moment.

MARGARET

Ted?

TED

Yes.

MARGARET

What's the problem?

TED

Well, admittedly, that was the best part of the night. It was pretty fuckin' cool, actually. But it was still an unnerving way to start off the night.

MARGARET

Sounds to me like a pretty great way to start off the night.

TED

Okay, let's just skip over the witches.

MARGARET

—Skipping over the witches.

TED

So, later, in another room, some crazy sucking maniac
sticks a gun in my face and forces me to play out some
psychosexual drama with his wife.

MARGARET

He made you have psycho sex with his wife?

TED

No, he didn't make me fuck his wife, he thought I'd fucked
his wife! He held me at gunpoint with a loaded gun!

MARGARET

What kinda gun?

TED

I don't know, I'm not a gun guy. It was big.

MARGARET

Like Dirty Harry's gun?

TED

Yeah, something like that.

MARGARET

Did it have a real long barrel or a short barrel?

TED

What difference does it make?

MARGARET

Well, for one thing it's the difference between a .44 Magnum and a Magnum .357.

TED

Who cares if it was a .44 or a .392, it was a fuckin' loaded gun, pointed at my fuckin' head!

Margaret takes this in.

MARGARET

You wanna skip over this part, too?

TED

I want you to get Betty on the phone!

MARGARET

Hold on.
                    (yelling to the room)
Anybody live here named . . .

MARGARET
                    (to Ted)
What's her name again?

TED

Betty

MARGARET

Betty!

The whole sleepy room stirs. Betty wakes up from the floor.

BETTY

Yeah, whatcha screamin' about?

MARGARET

You're Betty?

BETTY

Yeah, I'm Betty, it's my fuckin' place, who the fuck are you?

MARGARET

I'm Margaret
                    (hands her the phone)
And this is Ted.

Betty takes the phone.

BETTY

Ted, what's the problem?

TED

What's the *problem*? I don't got a *problem*, I got fuckin' *problems*! Wanna hear?

BETTY
              (yawning, wiping sleep from her eyes)
Sure.

TED

Well, most recently, there's room 716. There's a scary Mexican gangster dude pokin' his finger in my chest. There's his hooligan kids snapping their fingers at me. There's the putrid rotting corpse of a dead whore stuffed in the springs of a bed. There're rooms blazing afire. . . . There's a needle from God knows where stuck in my leg, infecting me with God knows what, and finally, there's me walking out the fuckin' door right now! *Buenas noches.*

A RINGING SOUND happens that we haven't heard before. Ted's head turns toward it.

It's the guest board. And the top light, the penthouse, is ringing.
It rings where all the others buzzed.

Betty can hear it distinctly on her side of the line. The sound fully
wakes her up. They start speaking Howard Hawks style again.

BETTY
(suddenly alert)
Is that the penthouse?

TED
Yeah.

BETTY
That's the Chester Rush party, they want something.

TED
Yeah, well, tough titty. They're just gonna have to wait,
'cause I'm out the door.

BETTY
(panicking)
Now, Ted, wait a minute. I know you're freaked, I know
you're stressed. You've had a real bad night—

TED
Yes, Betty, I've had-a-real-bad-night—

BETTY
—You say there's a dead body in a room?

TED
Yes, I did.

BETTY

No problem, this is a hotel, we've had dead bodies before, it's just the price of doing business. You said the hotel was on fire. Is it still on fire?

TED

No, it's out.

BETTY

Good, sprinkler system worked like a charm. Now, you wanna leave, you've had enough. Perfectly understandable. I'll take care of everything else. The only thing I ask is that you take care of Chester Rush. Then you can leave.

TED

Now, look—

BETTY

Ted, he's a very important guest of this hotel. In fact, he is the most important guest at the hotel. The Mon Signor used to be a haven for movie stars. Through the thirties and forties, and the first half of the fifties, more movie stars—if you break it down on a night-by-night basis—stayed at the Mon Signor than any other hotel in Hollywood. Now, we had some hard times in the eighties, even though we were the official hotel of Cannon Pictures, but we're coming back strong in the nineties. And a movie star clientele is important to that comeback. If we can keep stars of his magnitude happy, we're on our way. So, Ted, just take care of him, then you can leave.

TED

Look, I don't feel like—

BETTY

He probably just wants some champagne! You can do that, can't you? Please just take care of him, the entire staff of the Mon Signor is begging you!

Ted crumbles.

TED

Okay. But get your ass down here pronto.

BETTY

You're a good man, Ted. Thanks.

Ted hangs up the phone. And picks up the board phone.

TED

Hello, Mr. Rush. Sorry for the delay. How can I help you?

FADE TO BLACK

STORY TITLE CARD:

the penthouse

the man
from
hollywood

quentin
tarantino

■

EXT. HALLWAY TO PENTHOUSE—NIGHT

The elevator door opens and Ted wheels out his tray into the hallway.

There's been a bit of an effort to make himself appear a bit less disheveled than in the last scene. He's only minorly successful in the attempt. His uniform still looks like shit, his hair looks tousled, and he walks with a limp.

He wheels the cart up to the penthouse door and KNOCKS at the door.

A woman opens the door, it's Angela from Alex's story.

> ANGELA
>
> Hi, Theodore.

> TED
>
> What the hell are you doing here?

She holds up the drink she has in her hand.

> ANGELA
>
> Having a drink.

> TED
>
> Is that crazy husband of yours in there?

> ANGELA
>
> Are you kidding, he'll be asleep till Christmas.

From behind her we hear:

> VOICE (OS)

Entrez, entrez.

Angela steps aside and Ted wheels in the tray.

INT. PENTHOUSE—NIGHT

The penthouse is huge, far and away the best suite in the house. And standing in the middle of the biggest room in the hotel is the hottest, newest comedy star to burst onto the Hollywood scene in nearly a decade: Chester Rush. At this moment in time he's the king, and he has the swagger of a new king. After only one movie, he pulled the sword out of the stone. And the look on his face says, "King's good." Surrounding him is his entourage. They all look like once upon a time this evening they were dressed sharp; however, at this late hour everybody looks about as disheveled as Ted.

One of the lads, Norman, has planted roots in a comfy chair with his leg thrown over the arm and a bottle of Jim Beam in his hand.

The second guy, Leo, is in the back of the room pacing back and forth on the telephone. He is completely oblivious to the rest of the room's activity.

In Chester's hand is an ever present glass of champagne, which he constantly spills as he gestures wildly. Around the room are the leftovers: pizza boxes, fast-food hamburgers, and empty bottles of Cristal Champagne.

> CHESTER
> *(still sitting)*

Entrez, entrez, come in, come in.

                              TED
                    (wheeling in the tray)
Hi, sorry I took so long, but I got everything you asked
for—

                            CHESTER
—Not a problem, my friend Mr. Bellboy.

Angela, as she closes the door.

                            ANGELA
His name's Theodore.

                              TED
Actually, it's not Theodore,
                    (He throws a look at Angela)
It's Ted.

Chester rises from the couch.

                            CHESTER
So, Ted the Bellboy, as I was saying—would you care for
some champagne? That's not what I was saying, but would
you care for some champagne?

                              TED
No, thank you.

                            CHESTER
Ya sure? Cristal. It's the best. I never liked champagne
before I had Cristal, now I love it.

                              TED
Okay, yeah, sure.

As Chester goes and pours Ted a glass.

CHESTER

—As I was saying, Ted, don't worry about being late. For our purposes, promptness is far behind thoroughness.

On "thoroughness," he hands Ted the glass.

CHESTER

Chin-chin.

They clink glasses and drink.

CHESTER

Whadya say, Ted?

TED

Thank you?

CHESTER

No, not thank you. Whadya say about the tasty beverage?

TED

It's good.

CHESTER

Fuckin' good, Ted. It's *fuckin'* good. Let's try it again, shall we? So, Ted, whadya think about the beverage?

TED

It's fuckin' good.

CHESTER

You bet your sweet bippy, Ted. It's fuckin' Cristal, everything else is piss.

Norman in the chair starts yelling at Ted.

NORMAN

Bellboy! Bellboy! Bellboy!

Ted knows he's being laughed at, but not why.

CHESTER

(to Norman)

Knock it off, you're making' my friend Ted here uneasy.

(to Ted)

Pay no attention to Norman here, Ted, he's just fuckin' wit'
ya, that's all. That's from *Quadrophenia*.

Now me, myself, when I think of bellboys I think of—
"bellboy" isn't an insult, is it? Is there another name for
what you do that I'm ignorant of? Bellman, bellperson—

TED

Bellboy's fine.

CHESTER

Good. I'm glad they haven't changed that. There's a friend-
liness to "bellboy." As I was saying, Ted, when Norman
thinks of bellboys, he thinks of *Quadrophenia*. But me,
when I think of bellboys, I think of *The Bellboy*, with Jerry
Lewis. Didja ever see *The Bellboy*?

TED

No.

CHESTER

You should, it's one of Jerry's better movies. He never says
a word through the entire film. A completely silent perfor-
mance. How many actors can pull that off? And he has to
go to France to get respect. That says it all about America
right there. The minute Jerry Lewis dies, every paper in
this fuckin' country gonna write articles calling the man a

genius. It's not right. It's not right and it's not fair. But why should that surprise anybody? When has America ever been fair? We might be right every once in a while, but we're very rarely fair.

TED

Where do you want this?

CHESTER

You in a hurry, Ted?

TED

(He is, but doesn't want to rush the movie star)
No, not particularly.

CHESTER

Good, then stop playing "Beat the Clock." Now let me introduce you to everybody.

He puts his arm around Ted and leads him around the room.

Angela crosses frame, drink in hand.

CHESTER

Our friend from downstairs you already seem to be acquainted with.

As she snuggles up in a big comfy chair:

ANGELA

Oh, me and Theodore go way back. Don't we, Theodore?

TED

The name's Ted, Angela. I only let people with loaded guns at my head call me Theodore.

CHESTER

Angela's like you, Ted, a newfound friend.

ANGELA

We met at the pool.

CHESTER
(to Ted)

Have you ever seen Angela in a one-piece?

TED

No.

CHESTER

Well, it's somethin' to see.

CHESTER
(arm around Ted)

The Man sitting in the chair, with the bottle of Jim Beam in his hand and the sense of humor, is Norman. Norman, say hello to Ted.

NORMAN

What's up.

Norman shakes his hand.

CHESTER

The sociable son of a bitch on the telephone is Leo. And the person on the other end of the phone is his lovely wife Ellen.
(to Leo)

Leo, say hello to Ted.

Leo breaks away from his phone conversation for two seconds.

LEO

Hi, Ted, glad you could make it.

(back to phone)

What?

(pause)

What does punctuality have to do with love?

CHESTER

Which brings me to me, Chester Rush, Ted. Pleased to meetcha.

Chester shakes Ted's hand.

TED

I know. I'm sorry I haven't seen your movie.

Chester stops.

Ted wonders if he should have said that.

Chester walks over to the table and pours himself some more champagne. When he talks now it's slower and somewhat distracted. The tone of the scene starts changing.

CHESTER
It's quite all right, Ted, nothing to feel sorry about. That's why God invented video. But you know, Ted, a lot of people did see it.

Chester takes a drink of champagne, a disgusted look crosses his face, and he slowly puts it down.

His manner gives the room a chill.

When he talks, he addresses the room.

CHESTER
Who drank out of this bottle last?

No answer.

Chester walks over to Ted and fills his glass.

CHESTER
Who drank out of this bottle—not the other bottles—this bottle last?

NORMAN
What's wrong, Chester?

He spills the champagne from his glass on the floor.

CHESTER
It's fuckin' flat, Norman, that's what's wrong. The champagne—the fuckin' Cristal's fuckin' flat.

*Chester improvises a temper tantrum about the flat Cristal. Every-
one looks at him, not knowing what to say. Even Leo walks over
to witness. The whole room is uneasy and a little frightened.*

*When Chester finishes his tantrum, he turns his attention back to
Ted. As he talks to him, he opens up another bottle. But it's not
the rapid-pace delivery Chester has done so far. It's more troubled
and distracted.*

CHESTER
I was saying, Ted, a lot of people did see it. And not just on
video, either. Leo, what was the final take on domestic?

Leo is still in the doorway making sure his boy's cool.

LEO
72.1 million.
(worried tone)
You okay, champ?

CHESTER
(struggling with bottle)
I'm cool, so talk to your wife.

Leo turns his attention back to the phone and goes inside the room.

CHESTER
(to Ted)
72.1 million dollars. That's before video and before foreign,
and before pay-TV and before free TV. We're talking
fuckin' asses in fuckin' seats.
(He pops the cork)
Before all that other shit, *The Wacky Detective* made 72.1
million dollars.

Chester walks over to Ted and fills his glass.

CHESTER

And my new one, *The Dog Catcher*, it's projected to break
a hundred.

> *(He clinks Ted's glass with his)*

The Dog Catcher.

TED

The Dog Catcher.

They both drink.

*The tantrum's over, and Chester's back to his fast-talking, good-
natured self.*

CHESTER

Now let's stroll over here and see what goodies you brought
us.

TED

Do you mind me asking what's all this stuff for?

CHESTER

One thing at a time, Ted. I'm not a frog and you're not a
bunny, so let's not jump ahead. C'mon, Norman, you should
be interested in this.

NORMAN

Damn Skippy!

> *(pause)*

Tell it.

Ted produces the things they called for.

TED

A block of wood.

Chester knocks on it.

> CHESTER

Good.

> TED

Three nails.

> NORMAN

Why three nails?

> CHESTER

That's how many Peter Lorre asked for. Continue, Ted.

Ted is completely bewildered.

> TED

A roll of twine.

> CHESTER

That's definitely a roll of twine. Continue.

> TED

A bucket of ice.

> CHESTER
> *(to Norman)*

You into it?

> NORMAN
> *(to Chester)*

I'm into it.

> CHESTER
> *(to Ted)*

Go on.

                         TED

A donut.

Chester takes it and eats it.

                       CHESTER

That's for me. Continue.

                         TED

And a hatchet.

                       CHESTER

A hatchet sharp as the devil himself is what I asked for.

                         TED

Well, you be the judge.

*Ted holds the hatchet out for Chester to take. Norman snatches it
instead.*

                       NORMAN

I'll be the judge.

Norman touches the end of the blade with his thumb.

                       CHESTER

Whadya think?

                       NORMAN

That's a sharp motherfucker. Bring all this bullshit over to
the bar.

                       CHESTER

You heard him, Ted.

Ted is completely confused and starting to get a little scared, but he does what he's told.

Leo slams down the phone.

LEO

Bitch!

NORMAN

You still married?

LEO

Maybe, maybe not, but I don't give a flyin' fuck either way. I've had it with that Machiavellian bitch! I'm too drunk to drive home. I'm sorry about that, I'm real sorry about that. I got drunk on New Year's Eve, cut my fuckin' head off . . .
(noticing Ted at the bar)
What's going on here?

CHESTER

We now return you to *The Man from Rio*, already in progress.

LEO

(surprised)
Noooo, you're gonna do it?

NORMAN

Looks like.

LEO

You guys ain't bullshittin', you're gonna really go for it?

Angela is still curled up.

ANGELA

After talkin' about it all night, they better. I wanna see a show.

CHESTER

When we do it, you'll have something to see.

Leo walks up to Norman and throws his arm around him.

LEO

You are one radical dude.

Ted doesn't know what anybody's talking about, which is just fine with him. He finishes laying out everything on the bar and says:

TED

Well, that's everything, so if you don't need me for anything else, I'll go back downstairs.

CHESTER

Not so fast, Ted. We ain't quite done yet. Why don't you take a seat at the bar, get comfortable, and have an open mind when we explain the festivities of the evening to you.

TED

Look, guys, you paid for the room. As long as you don't break up the furniture, you can do whatever the fuck you want. And me personally, I don't care if you break up the furniture. You don't have to explain anything to me. Whatever constitutes a good time as far as you guys are concerned is your business.

CHESTER

Well, it's your business too, Ted. 'Cause we want you to take part.

TED

Take part in what?

LEO

Chester, your way of breaking the news to him gently is scarin' the shit outta him.

ANGELA

Look at the poor guy. Just spit it out.

Little by little everybody has gathered around Ted.

CHESTER

First off, let me say that there's nothing homosexual about what we're going to ask you to do. There's nothing sexual at all about what we want. But I was thinkin' you might be thinkin' we want you to do some sex thing. Pee on us, suck us off, shit like that. Let me assure you nothing could be farther from what we want

Angela interrupts:

ANGELA

Can I jump in here?

CHESTER

No, you can't jump in here, this is my story.

ANGELA

Theodore's been here fifteen minutes and you've talked about everything but.

CHESTER

Hey, if you don't like it, you can get the fuck out.

Leo taps his champagne glass with a tiny spoon, shutting every-body up.

LEO

If it'll please the court, let me explain to Ted our intentions.

NORMAN
(yelling)

I second the nomination!

CHESTER
(yelling)

Move the nomination be closed!

Chester takes the hatchet and brings it down on the bar like a gavel.

CHESTER
(calmly)

Leo, the floor is yours.

LEO

Thank you.
(to Ted)
Ted, did you ever watch the old "Alfred Hitchcock Show"?

TED
(totally bewildered at this point)

Yeah.

LEO

Did you ever see the episode *The Man from Rio*, with Peter Lorre and Steve McQueen?

TED

I don't think so.

LEO

Oh, you'd remember it all right. In the show, Peter Lorre
makes a bet that Steve McQueen can't light his cigarette
lighter ten times in a row. Now if Steve McQueen can light
his cigarette lighter ten times in a row, he wins Peter Lorre's new car. If he can't, he loses his little finger.

(pause)

Norman and Chester just made the same bet.

(pause)

Norman's putting up his pinky against Chester's mint con-
dition, 1964 red convertible Chevy Chevelle that he can
light his Zippo ten times in a row.

Pause.

Ted looks at all of them, taking in the information, before saying:

TED

You guys are drunk.

CHESTER

Well, that goes without saying, but that doesn't mean we
don't know what we're doing.

NORMAN

I'll tell ya what I'm doin'.

Norman lays an issue of Hot Classic Cars *in front of Ted on the
bar. On the cover is a picture of Chester smiling, standing next to
a beautiful 1964 red convertible Chevy Chevelle. The headline
reads: "Hollywood's Hottest New Star Next to America's Hottest
Old Car."*

NORMAN

I drive a motherfuckin' Honda my sister sold me. You hear
what I'm sayin'? A little white motherfuckin' Honda Civic.

> *(He holds up the magazine)*

You see this shit!

> *(Reading the magazine)*

"Hollywood's hottest new star, next to America's hottest old car."

> *(He hands Ted the magazine)*

Now you take a good look at that machine that this mother-fucker over here is standing next to. That's a 1964 nigger-red, rag-top Chevy Chevelle. And I love that car more'n I love hips, lips, and fingertips. Cut to we sittin' here celebrating, gettin' high, drinkin' champagne—

CHESTER

—Cristal. When you're drinkin' anything else, you're drinking champagne. When you're drinkin' Cristal, you say you're drinkin' Cristal.

NORMAN

—drinking Cristal. Watchin' TV. "Rockin' New Year's Eve." When all of a sudden we flip on Steve McQueen and Peter Lorre bein' fuckin' badass. And I look at this funny motherfucker over here, and I say, "I'd do that for the Chevelle."

LEO

And Chester replies . . .

CHESTER

". . . Oh, really?"

TED

You guys wouldn't be doin' something this stupid unless you were drunk.

Everybody breaks into a "here, here" murmur.

NORMAN

I think that pretty much goes without sayin'. We'd probably chicken out. But when you're fucked-up, you don't lie. You tell the fuckin' truth. And the fuckin' truth is, my lucky Zippo's gonna win me Chester's car.

TED

(to Chester)

Why are you doing this?

CHESTER

Thrill of the bet. I'm the one with something to lose here. 'Cause I can pretty near guarantee that I love my car more'n Norman loves his pinky.

TED

(to Leo)

How 'bout you guys, you're just gonna sit back and let your friends mutilate each other?

LEO

Why not? Life don't get much more exciting than this. I mean if Norman was puttin' his dick on the choppin' block, I'd step in, 'cause, ya know in the morning, we'd really regret that. But his pinky? Who gives a fuck? I mean theoretically, he could lose that choppin' onions tomorrow. Life still goes on.

TED

(to Angela)

How 'bout you?

ANGELA

(to Ted)

I don't care.

CHESTER

Which brings us to your part in this little wager.

TED

I don't have a part.

CHESTER

Now, Ted, my old granddaddy used ta say: "The less a man
makes declarative statements, the less he's apt to look fool-
ish in retrospect." Now there're some inherent obstacles in
this undertaking. First of all, I'm not some sick fuck like
Peter Lorre on that show, travelin' the countryside collect-
ing fingers. We're all buddies, here. Nobody wants Norman
to lose his finger. We just wanna chop it off. So if fate
doesn't smile on ol' Norman, we'll put his finger on ice and
rush 'im to a hospital, where they'll in all likelihood be able
to sew it back on.

TED

Hopefully.

LEO

Eighty percent.

NORMAN

Our side.

CHESTER

So Norman's protected. His interests have been looked
after. My interests, on the other hand, have not. I am as
emotionally attached to my car as Norman is physically to
his finger. I'm putting up a very expensive piece of machin-
ery on this wager. Now, if I lose, I lose, I have no problem
with that. I'm a big boy, I knew what I was doing. However,
if I win, I wanna win. If Norman lights his lighter ten times
in a row, he's gonna have no emotional problems about
taking my car keys whatsoever. But if I win, it's not incon-
ceivable that Leo or myself, at the last minute, might not be
able to wield the ax. Which brings us full circle to you,
Ted. Sober Ted. Clear-eyed Ted. We want you to be the
diceman.

Pause as they all look at him. Angela breaks it.

ANGELA

Helluva night, huh, Ted?

TED

I gotta get out of here.

Ted abruptly gets up and makes a beeline for the door.

*Chester whips out a hundred-dollar bill and quickly calls to Ted
from his position at the bar.*

CHESTER

Ted, I got a hundred-dollar bill here with your name on it, whether you do what we ask or not, just to sit back down in the chair for one minute more.

Ted spins in his direction.

TED

I'm not gonna cut off his finger!

CHESTER

Maybe you will and maybe you won't, but that has nothing to do with this hundred-dollar bill in my hand. You can tell us all to go fuck off and walk right out through that door. But if you sit back down and wait sixty seconds before you do it, you'll be a hundred dollars richer.

Ted just stands across the room, thinking.

ANGELA

Ted. Take the money.

LEO

Ted, you're gonna do whatever you want to do. We're just askin' you to indulge us for another minute more. And Chester's willin' to pay for it.

Ted thinks.

TED

I'll take your money, and I'll sit back down. But a minute from now, I'm gonna walk out the door, and when I do, there'll be no hard feelings?

CHESTER

Well, I want you to have a bit more of an open mind than that, but, yeah, we'll either convince you or we won't. No hard feelings. Right, guys?

Everybody agrees.

Ted wearily sits back down.

Chester positions himself in front of Ted at the bar.

CHESTER

Okay, Leo, you be the timekeeper. Let us know when one minute begins and when it ends.

LEO

You got it.
                    (He checks his watch)
Gentlemen, start up your engines.

Chester jumps up and down, loosening up.

LEO

Begin!

Chester, who talks fast anyway, starts his pitch. It's Chester who now plays "Beat the Clock."

CHESTER

Okay, pay attention here, Ted, I ain't got much time. Now I'm gonna make two piles here on the bar.
(He takes the hundred-dollar bill and lays it out on the bar)
One pile,
(pointing at the hundred-dollar bill)
which is yours. And another pile,
(Chester whips out a money roll fat enough to choke a horse to death)
which could be yours.
(He lays a matching hundred-dollar bill on the bar, starting his second pile)
Now, what you have to be aware of is we're gonna do this bet, one way,
(He lays another hundred on the end pile)
or the other.
(He lays another hundred on the pile)
Whether it's you who holds the ax,
(he lays another hundred on the pile)
or the desk clerk downstairs,
(he lays another hundred on the pile)
or some bum we yank off the street.
(He lays another hundred on the pile) . . .

NORMAN

You can buy a lot of soup with that pile.

CHESTER

(to Norman)
Shhhh, I'm the closer.
(to the group)
How much is on the bar already? I lost count.

ANGELA

Six hundred.

CHESTER

Six hundred. Ted, do you know how long it takes the aver-
age American to count to six hundred?

TED

No.

CHESTER
(laying another bill on the pile)
One minute less than it takes to count to seven hundred.
You know, Ted, a person's life is made up of a zillion little
experiences.
(He lays another bill on the pile)
Some, which have no meaning, are insignificant and you
forget them. And some that stick with you for the rest of
your natural life—
(he lays another bill on the pile)
—barring Alzheimer's of course. Now, what we're propos-
ing is so unusual, so outside the norm, that I think it would
be a pretty good guess that this will be one of those experiences that *sticks*. So, since you're gonna be *stuck* remember-
ing this moment for the rest of your life, you gotta decide
what that memory will be.
(He lays down the last bill on the pile)
So, are you gonna remember for the next forty years, give
or take a decade, how you refused a thousand dollars for
one second's worth of work, or how you made a thousand
dollars for one second's worth of work?

LEO

Time!

                    CHESTER
Well, Ted, what's it gonna be?

Ted looks at the pile, then looks up. We dolly into his face.

FLASHBACK

We see a quick MONTAGE *of horrendous moments from all the other stories*

INT. PENTHOUSE—NIGHT

Back to Ted.

                    TED
    Okay.

The group cheers.

                    TED
    But when it's over, no matter what happens, I get the
    money?

                    CHESTER
    As long as you do your part, you can take the pile, walk out
    the door, and not say another word.

                    TED
    Let's do it right now, before I change my mind.

                    NORMAN
Here, here.

Everybody gets in their position by the bar. Norman lays his left hand on the block of wood with his pinky sticking out.

In his right hand is his Zippo lighter, poised and ready to strike.

Chester hands Ted the meat cleaver.

Ted takes it, raises it up above Norman's finger, in position.

CHESTER
Perfect, perfect, perfect, perfect! This is great! This is a moment in time none of us will ever forget.

Everybody is crowded around the scene, on pins and needles.

CHESTER
Norman, you ready?

NORMAN
Ready!

CHESTER

Ted, you ready?

TED

Ready.

CHESTER

Okeydoke. Norman, begin.

Norman looks hard at the Zippo in his hand. Ted, holding the cleaver, stares focused on Norman's pinky.

Norman readies himself.

Places his thumb on the wheel in the Zippo.

Takes a breath.

And strikes.

It sparks, but doesn't light.

Without missing a beat, Ted brings down the cleaver, slicing off Norman's pinky.

Norman lets out a scream.

Ted, in one move, lays down the cleaver, scoops up the money, and walks out the door.

INT. HALLWAY—AFTER DAWN

CAMERA is positioned at far end of hallway, looking down it at the elevator at the other end.

Ted walks out of the penthouse in the f.g. In a MEDIUM SHOT, he takes the thousand dollars in his hand, looks at it, smiles, and sticks it in his pocket. It might've been a bad night, but it's been a profitable one. He chuckles at the irony and, whistling a happy tune, turns his back on the camera and walks down the hall to the elevator.

All the while we hear PANDEMONIUM breaking out behind the door.

As Ted walks to the elevator, the CREDITS ROLL. He waits for the elevator, it arrives, he gets in, the doors close.

As CREDITS CONTINUE TO ROLL, we hold for about two beats . . . then . . .

The Door BURSTS open and everybody comes piling out. Everybody's screaming, yelling different things to one another. Norman has a bloody towel wrapped around his hand, he's screaming and crying.

NORMAN
My finger, my fucking finger!!

Chester has the bucket of ice with the finger in it. Leo's trying to direct everything. Everybody's in frantic activity, except for Angela, who stands back, drinks her drink, and watches the show. They all run down the hall, toward the elevator. Somebody trips and they all hit the ground. The bucket of ice with the finger goes spilling. They run around like crazy, looking for the finger and picking up ice cubes. Norman lies on the floor and screams. They pick it all up, get to the elevator, and push the button.

When it arrives, they all dive in except for Angela.

ANGELA
You know, I'm gonna call it a night and go back to my room. It's been fun.

The doors close on the screaming maniacs.

Angela walks through a door marked "Stairway."

INT. 4TH FLOOR HALLWAY—AFTER DAWN

MEDIUM STAIRWAY DOOR

CREDIT ROLL continues

Angela comes through the door; we STEADICAM in front of her as she walks the halls, looking for her room. She finds it . . .

WE STOP CREDITS

four rooms

Angela sticks her key in the door, then stops when she sees something approaching. The look on her face combines strange awe and mild shock.

Almost floating ethereally, a mysterious Blond Bombshell, wearing Diana's see-through negligée and slippers, armed with Elspeth's sword slung over her shoulder, wanders toward her. She is in a daze, perhaps drunk or lost.

> ANGELA
>
> You okay, lady?

The bombshell looks up at her dizzily.

> ANGELA
>
> I said—you looking for someone?

> DIANA
> *(disoriented)*
> Uhhh . . . yes . . . my husband . . . I think. Have you seen him?

Angela and the girl have a strange moment as they connect through the eyes. Having had enough intensity tonight, Angela breaks their eye contact.

> ANGELA
>
> Lady, I haven't seen anybody.

Diana quietly says, "Ohhh," as she drifts on down the hall in a daze. Angela puts her hand to her temples before opening her hotel door. She does a double-take on the hallway—empty.

She pauses a beat, then walks into her room. After the door closes, we hear Sigfried on the other side.

SIGFRIED
Where the hell have you been?

CREDITS CONTINUE TO ROLL

credits
and
cast list

Miramax Films Presents

■

A Band Apart

■

A film by
Allison Anders
Alexandre Rockwell
Robert Rodriguez
Quentin Tarantino

Tim Roth as "Ted the Bellhop"

Antonio Banderas
Jennifer Beals
Paul Calderon
Sammi Davis
Amanda deCadenet
Valeria Golino
Kathy Griffin
Marc Lawrence
Madonna
David Proval
Ione Skye
Quentin Tarantino
Lili Taylor
Marisa Tomei
Tamlyn Tomita
Alicia Witt

■

Introducing
Lana McKissack
Danny Verduzco

■

Costume Designers
Susan L. Bertram
Mary Claire Hannan

■

Music by
Combustible Edison

■

Music Produced by
Mark Mothersbaugh

■

Production Designer
Gary Frutkoff

■

Editors
Margie Goodspeed
Elena Maganini
Sally Menke
Robert Rodriguez

■

Directors of Photography
Rodrigo Garcia
Guillermo Navarro
Phil Parmet
Andrzej Sekula

■

Co-Producers
Paul Hellerman
Heidi Vogel

Scott Lambert

▪

Executive Producers
Alexandre Rockwell
Quentin Tarantino

▪

Written By
Allison Anders
Alexandre Rockwell
Robert Rodriguez
Quentin Tarantino

▪

Produced By
Lawrence Bender

STRANGE BREW

▪

Written and Directed By
Allison Anders

▪

Cast
Sammi Davis Jezebel
Amanda deCadenet Diana

Valeria Golino **Athena**
Madonna **Elspeth**
Ione Skye **Eva**
Lili Taylor **Raven**
Alicia Witt **Kiva**

▪

Director of Photography
Rodrigo Garcia

▪

Editor
Margie Goodspeed

THE WRONG MAN

▪

Written and Directed by
Alexandre Rockwell

▪

Cast
Jennifer Beals **Angela**
David Proval **Sigfried**

▪

Director of Photography
Phil Parmet

▪

Editor
Elena Maganini

THE MISBEHAVERS

■

Written and Directed by
Robert Rodriguez

■

Cast

Antonio Banderas	**Man**
Lana McKissack	**Sarah**
Patricia Vonne Rodriguez	**Corpse**
Tamlyn Tomita	**Wife**
Danny Verduzco	**Juancho**
Salma Hayek	**TV Dancing Girl**

■

Director of Photography
Guillermo Navarro

■

Editor
Robert Rodriguez

THE MAN FROM HOLLYWOOD

■

Written and Directed by
Quentin Tarantino

■

Cast

Jennifer Beals	**Angela**
Paul Calderon	**Norman**
Quentin Tarantino	**Chester**

■

Director of Photography
Andrzej Sekula

■

Steadicam Operator
Bob Gorelick

■

Editor
Sally Menke

Lawrence Bender	**Long Hair Yuppie Scum**
Kathy Griffin	**Betty**
Paul Hellerman	**Taxi Driver**
Quinn Thomas Hellerman	**Baby Bellhop**
Marc Lawrence	**Sam the Bellhop**
Unruly Julie McClean	**Left Redhead**
Laura Rush	**Right Redhead**
Paul Skemp	**Real Theodore**
Marisa Tomei	**Margaret**

and
Tim Roth as "Ted the Bellhop"

■

Stunt Players
Kane Hodder
Alan Marcus
Charles Belardinelli
Tom Bellissimo

■

Production Manager	**Paul Hellerman**
Production Supervisor	**Deborah Cass**
1st Assistant Director	**Douglas Aarniokoski**

"Strange Brew" & "Misbehavers"

1st Assistant Director *"The Wrong Man"* & *"The Man From Hollywood"*	**Fernando Altschul**
2nd Assistant Directors	**Brian Bettwy** **Louis Shaw Milito**
Production Accountant	**Deborah Hebert**
Assistant Accountant	**Heidrun M. Williams**
Accounting Assistant	**Craig Roth**
Production Coordinator	**Dawn Todd**
Asst. Production Coordinator	**Susan Noonan-Gero**
Key Office Production Assistant	**Jeff Swafford**
Script Supervisor	**Jayne-Ann Tenggren**
Location Manager	**Robert Earl Craft**
Camera Operator/1st Assistant Camera	**Ziad Doueiri**
2nd Assistant Camera	**Gregory Smith**
1st Assistant "B" Camera	**Kate Butler**
2nd Assistant "B" Camera	**Bjorn E. Aarskog**
Steadicam Operator *"The Wrong Man"* & *"Misbehavers"*	**Jonathan Brown**
Production Sound Mixer	**Pawel Wdowczak**
Boom Operator	**Paul Koronkiewicz**
Key Hair/Make-Up Artist *"Misbehavers"* & *"The Man From Hollywood"*	**Ermahn Ospina**
Assistant Hair and Make-Up *"Misbehavers"* & *"The Man From Hollywood"*	**Don Malot**
Co-Key Make-Up *"The Man From Hollywood"*	**Cristina Bartolucci**

Key Make-Up *"Strange Brew"* & *"The Wrong Man"* **Lizbeth Williamson**

Key Hair *"Strange Brew"* & *"The Wrong Man"* **Michael Ross**

Assistant Make-Up *"Strange Brew"* **Toni G.**

Assistant Hair *"Strange Brew"* **Barbara Olvera**

Make-up for Madonna **Paul Starr**

Hairstylist for Madonna **Orlando**

Hairstylist for Bruce Willis **Pamela Priest**

Wigmaker **Ira Senz Company**

Costume Supervisor *"Strange Brew"* & *"Misbehavers"* **Thomas G. Marquez**

Costume Supervisor *"The Wrong Man"* & *"The Man From Hollywood"* **Jacqueline Aronson**

Costumer **Mynka Draper**

Gaffer **Chuck Smith**

Best Boy Electric **Edgar Arellano**

Electricians **Jason Lord**
Heather Hillmeyer
Marcel De Jure

Key Grip **Rick Stribling**

Best Boy Grip **James B. "Crash" Irons**

Dolly Grip **Bob Ivanjack**

Grips **Jason "Jake" Cross**
Tim "Stuffy" Soronen
Marc Thomas Polanski
Elizabeth Bolden

Art Director **Mayne Schuyler Berke**

Set Director	**Sara Andrews**
Lead Man	**Peter Borck**
Construction Coordinator	**Brian Markey**
Property Master	**Lynda Reiss**
Assistant Property Master	**Andrew King**
On-Set Dresser	**Francis Whitebloom**
Assistant Decorator	**Mary Patvaldnieks**
Art Department Coordinator	**Marisol Jimenez**
Swing Gang	**Joseph Grafmuller** **Steven Ingrassia** **Randy Tenhaeff** **Thomas J. Power**
Draper	**Shari Griffin**
Construction Foreman	**Ray Maxwell**
Lead Carpenter	**Shane Hawkins**
Construction Estimator	**Chris Scher**
Carpenters	**James C. Beeson** **Dave Edinger** **Brant R. McCarthy** **Mark Peters** **Mark F. Simpson** **Floyd Valero**
On-Set Carpenter	**James M. Drury Jr.**
Lead Painter	**Mark D. Gillson**
Painters	**Adam G. Markey** **Pedro V. Suchite** **Carlos A. Chavez**
Stand-By Painter	**T. D. Donnelly**
1st Assistant Editors	
"Strange Brew"	**Bob Allen** **Debra L. Tennant**
"The Wrong Man"	**David Young**
"The Misbehavers"	**Erik C. Andersen**
"The Man From Hollywood"	**Tatiana S. Riegel**

2nd Assistant Editors	
"Strange Brew"	**Johanna Groepl**
"The Wrong Man"	**Steven M. Buono**
"The Misbehavers"	**Daniel A. Fort**
"The Man From Hollywood"	**Katie Mack**
Additional Assistant Editor	**Don Likovich**
Apprentice Editors	**Ethan Maniquis**
	Joaquin Avellan
Music Editor	**Denise Okimoto**
	Pacific Music Editors, Inc.
Video Playback	**Playback Technologies**
Unit Publicist	**Nancy Willen**
Unit Still Photographer	**Claudette Barius**
Casting By	**Russell Gray**
Casting Associate	**Randi Hiller**
Extras Casting By	**Rainbow Casting**
Stand-Ins	**Michael Boyce Harris**
	Lisa Redding
Assistant to Mr. Bender	**Courtney McDonnell**
Assistant to Ms. Anders	**Melanie Chapman**
Assistant to Mr. Rockwell	**Amanda M. Michener**
Assistant to Mr. Tarantino	**Victoria Lucai**
Coordinator for Miramax	**Cathy Agcayab**
A Band Apart Legal	**Carlos Goodman, Eric Brooks**
	LICHTER, GROSSMAN & NICHOLS, INC.
Music Legal Services	**Myman, Abell, Fineman,**
	Greenspan & Rowan
Miramax Legal	**Vicki Cherkas**
Completion Guarantors	**Film Finances, Inc.,**
	Kurt Woolner
	Maureen Duffy
Set Production Assistants	**Ben Parker**
	Karen Alicia White

Office Production Assistants	**Charles Sapadin**
	Canard Emile Barnes
Intern	**Tiffanie DeBartolo**
Transportation Coordinator	**P. Gerald Knight**
Transportation Captain	**Dotti Thompson**
Drivers	**Geoff Lancaster**
	D. Robert Knight
Animal Trainers	**McMillan Animal Rentals**
	Brian McMillan
Choreographer	**Sissy Boyd**
Medic/Stage Manager	**Patrice Carbaugh**
Studio Teacher	**Jan D. Tys**
Set Security by	**Technical Guard Security**
	NICK ROBERTS, SUPERVISOR
Production Catering by	**Silver Screen Catering**
Craft Service	**Derek Hurd**
Special Mechanical Effects	**Bellisimo/Bellardinelli Effects, Inc.**
Special Effects Assistants	**Shannon Thompson**
	Christy Sumner
Special Make-Up Effects by	**K.N.B. EFX Group, Inc.**
Post Production Accountant	**Zane**
Post Production Coordinators	**Dawn Todd**
	Alyson Evans
Post Production Assistants	**Ben Parker**
	Jeff Swafford
Supervising Sound Editors	**Bruce Fortune M.P.S.E.**
	Victor Iorillo M.P.S.E.
Supervising ADR Editor	**Becky Sullivan M.P.S.E.**
Sound FX Editors	**Glenn Hoskinson**
	Donald L. Warner, Jr. M.P.S.E.
	Shawn Sykora M.P.S.E.

Anthony R. Milch
Howard Neiman
Bernard Weiser M.P.S.E.

Special Sound Effects Victor Iorillo M.P.S.E.

1st Assistant Sound Editor Tim Tuchrello

2nd Assistant Sound Editor Vincent Casarro

ADR Editor Zack Davis

Supervising Foley Editor Gordon Ecker M.P.S.E.

Sound Effects Recordists Gary Blufer

Sound Effects Coordinators John Michael Fanaris
Blake Marion
Dawn Kratofil

Re-Recording Mixers Wayne Heitman
Tom Dahl

Re-Recording Mixer B. Tennyson Sebastian III
"The Misbehavers"

ADR Voice Casting Barbara Harris

ADR Mixer Christina Tucker

Negative Cutter Theresa Repola Mohammed

Color Timer Michael Stanwick

Dolby Stereo Consultant Thom "Coach" Ehle

Music Consultant Karyn Rachtman
Mary Ramos
Kristen Becht

Music Engineer Robert Casale

Music Recorded by Mutato Muzika

"Carnival of Souls"	Theme From "The Tiki Wonder Hour"
Written by: Peter Dixon	Written by: Peter Dixon
Performed by: Combustible Edison	Performed by: Combustible Edison
Courtesy of: Sub Pop Records	Courtesy of: Sub Pop Records

"Breakfast at Denny's" "The Millionaire's Holiday"
Written by: Peter Dixon Written by: Peter Dixon,
                          Elizabeth Cox
Performed by: Combustible Edison Performed by: Combustible
                          Edison
Courtesy of: Sub Pop Records Courtesy of: Sub Pop Records

"Spy Vs. Spy" "Harlem Nocturne"
Written by: Michael Cudahy Written by: Earle Hagen
Performed by: Combustible Edison Performed by: Esquivel
Courtesy of: Sub Pop Records Courtesy of: The RCA Records
                          Label of BMG Music

"Sentimental Journey" "Bewitched (Theme Song)"
Written by: Bud Green, Written by: Jack Keller, Howard
Les Brown, Ben Homer Greenfield
Performed by: Esquivel Courtesy of: Tee Vee Toons
Courtesy of: The RCA Records
Label of BMG Music

"YMCA"
Written by: Jacques Morali, Henri Belolo, Victor Willis
Performed by: The Village People
Courtesy of: Mercury Records by Arrangement with
Polygram Special Markets/Scorpio Music and Can't Stop Music

Executive in Charge of Soundtrack for Elektra Entertainment
Andrew Leary

Original Motion Picture Soundtrack Album Available on Elektra
Compact Discs and Cassettes

Featuring New Music from Combustible Edison

Special Thanks To:
Agnes b.
Stephanie Allain
Maureen Angelinetta
Lola Babalon
Pamela Barish
Hugo Boss
Zoe Cassavetes
Champagne Louis Roederer S.A.
Claire Chew
Chris Connelly

Roald Dahl
Dolce & Gabbana
Donna Karan Menswear
Emporio Armani
Giorgio Armani
Guinness Distillers
Hama Design
Leland H. Faust
Jim Hannafin
Lisa Henson
Eddie Tishkoff, Hollywood Piano Co.
Jerry Lewis
Lawrence Lorre
Adam Lustig
Gerald Martinez
Sean McCleese
Joel Millner
Mike Simpson
Maya Montanez Smukler
Cindy Jo Stanberry
Lee Stollman
Shelley Surpin
Frank Tashlin
Jamie Toscas
United Independent Taxi
Bumble Ward
Kurt Voss

Specialty Prop Fabrication by
Lowtech
Adam deFelice
Matthew Gratzner

Travel Arrangements & Services Provided by
Judy Garland and Associates

Stock Footage Provided by
Producers Library Service &
Film & Video Stock Shots, Inc.

Electric Equipment Provided by
S.I.R. Studios

Grip Equipment Provided by
Cinelease

Cameras and Lenses Provided by
Panavision Hollywood

Camera Dolly Provided by
J. L. Fisher

Opticals by
Pacific Title

Visual Effects by
Jay Mark Johnson
Bertha Garcia
Design and Animation

Robert Stromberg
David S. Williams Jr.
Illusion Arts, Inc.
Joe Gareri
Patrick Phillips
Pacific Title Digital

Animated Titles Created by
Bob Kurtz

Animation Produced by
Kurtz and Friends

Creative Consultant
Chuck Jones

Animators
Pam Cooke-Weiner
Shane Zalvin
Gary Mooney
Dave Spafford

Titles by
Pittard-Sullivan-Fitzgerald

Post Production Sound by
Soundstorm®

Insurance Provided by
Great Northern / Reiff & Associates

Originated on Eastman® Color Negative

Color by
Deluxe®

Recorded in Dolby® Stereo

Filmed With Panavision®
Cameras & Lenses